The Governors

by

E. Phillips Oppenheim

Double 9
BOOKS

The Governors
by E. Phillips Oppenheim

ISBN: 978-93-57273-11-4

Published by

DOUBLE 9 BOOKS

2/13-B, Ansari Road
Daryaganj, New Delhi – 110002
info@double9books.com
www.double9books.com
Tel. 011-40042856

ABOUT THE AUTHOR

E. Phillips Oppenheim was born on October 22, 1866, in Tohhenham, London, England, to Henrietta Susannah Temperley Budd and Edward John Oppenheim, a leather retailer. After leaving school at age 17, he helped his father in his leather business and used to write in his extra time. His first novel, Expiration (1886), and subsequent thrillers piqued the interest of a wealthy New York businessman who eventually bought out the leather business and made Oppenheim a high-paid director.He is more focused on dedicating most of his time to writing. The novels, volumes of short stories, and plays that followed, numbering more than 150, were about humans with modern heroes, fearless spies, and stylish noblemen. The Long Arm of Mannister (1910), The Moving Finger (1911), and The Great Impersonation (1920) are three of his most famous essays.

CONTENTS

BOOK I

CHAPTER I.
MR. PHINEAS DUGE

Virginia, when she had torn herself away from the bosom of her sorrowing but excited family, and boarded the car which passed only once a day through the tiny village in Massachusetts, where all her life had been spent, had felt herself, notwithstanding her nineteen years, a person of consequence and dignity. Virginia, when four hours later she followed a tall footman in wonderful livery through a stately suite of reception rooms in one of the finest of Fifth Avenue mansions, felt herself suddenly a very insignificant person. The roar and bustle of New York were still in her ears. Bewildered as she had been by, this first contact with all the distracting influences of a great city, she was even more distraught by the wonder and magnificence of these, her more immediate surroundings. She, who had lived all her life in a simple farmhouse, where every one worked, and a single servant was regarded as a luxury, found herself suddenly in the palace of a millionaire, a palace made perfect by the despoilment of more than one of the most ancient homes in Europe.

Very timidly, and with awed glances, she looked around her as she was conducted in leisurely manner to the sanctum of the great man at whose bidding she had come. The pictures on the walls, magnificent and impressive even to her ignorant eyes; the hardwood floors, the wonderful furniture, the statuary and flowers, the smooth-tongued servants—all these things were an absolute revelation to her. She had read of such things, even perhaps dreamed of them, but she had never imagined it possible that she herself might be brought into actual contact with them.

At every step she took she felt her self-confidence decreasing; her clothes, made by the village dressmaker from an undoubted

French model, with which she had been more than satisfied only a few hours ago, seemed suddenly dowdy and ill-fashioned. She was even doubtful about her looks, although quite half a dozen of the nicest young men in her neighbourhood had been doing their best to make her vain since the day when she had left college, an unusually early graduate, and returned to her father's tiny home to become the acknowledged belle of the neighbourhood. Here, though, she felt her looks of small avail; she might reign as a queen in Wellham Springs, but she felt herself a very insignificant person in the home of her uncle, the great railway millionaire and financier, Mr. Phineas Duge. Her courage had almost evaporated when at last, after a very careful knock at the door, an English footman ushered her into the small and jealously guarded sanctum in which the great man was sitting. She passed only a few steps across the threshold, and stood there, a timid, hesitating figure, her dark eyes very anxiously searching the features of the man who had risen from his seat to greet her.

"So this is my niece Virginia," he said, holding out both his hands. "I am glad to see you. Take this chair close to me. I am getting an old man, you see, and I have many whims. I like to have any one with whom I am talking almost at my elbow. Now tell me, my dear, what sort of a journey you have had. You look a little tired, or is it because everything here is strange to you?"

All her fears seemed to be melting away. Never could she have imagined a more harmless-looking, benevolent, and handsome old gentleman. He was thin and of only moderate stature. His white hair, of which he still had plenty, was parted in the middle and brushed away in little waves. He was clean-shaven, and his grey eyes were at once soft and humorous. He had a delicate mouth, refined features, and his slow, distinct speech was pleasant, almost soothing to listen to. She felt suddenly an immense wave of relief, and she realized perhaps for the first time how much she had dreaded this meeting.

"I am not really tired at all," she assured him, "only you see I have never been in a big city, and it is very noisy here, isn't it? Besides, I have never seen anything so beautiful as this house. I think it frightened me a little."

He laid his hand upon hers kindly.

"I imagine," he said, smiling, "that you will very soon get used to this. You will have the opportunity, if you choose."

She laughed softly.

"If I choose!" she repeated. "Why, it is all like fairyland to me."

He nodded.

"You come," he said, "from a very quiet life. You will find things here different. Do you know what these are?"

He touched a little row of black instruments which stood on the top of his desk. She shook her head doubtfully.

"I am not quite sure," she admitted.

"They are telephones," he said. "This one"—touching the first—"is a private wire to my offices in Wall Street. This one"—laying a finger upon the second—"is a private wire to the bank of which I am president. These two," he continued, "are connected with the two brokers whom I employ. The other three are ordinary telephones—two for long distance calls and one for the city. When you came in I touched this knob on the floor beneath my foot. All the telephones were at once disconnected here and connected with my secretaries' room. I can sit here at this table and shake the money-markets of the world. I can send stocks up or down at my will. I can ruin if I like, or I can enrich. It is the fashion nowadays to speak lightly of the mere man of money, yet there is no king on his throne who can shake the world as can we kings of the money-market by the lifting even of a finger."

"Are you a millionaire?" she asked timidly. "But, of course, you must be, or you could not live in a house like this."

He laid his hand gently upon hers.

"Yes," he said, "I am a millionaire a good many times over, or I should not be of much account in New York. But there, I have told you enough about myself. I sent for you, as you know, because there are times when I feel a little lonely, and I thought that if my sister could spare one of her children, it would be a kindly act, and one which I might perhaps be able to repay. Do you think that you would like to live here with me, Virginia, and be mistress of this house?"

She shrank a little away. The prospect was not without its terrifying side.

"Why, I should love it," she declared, "but I simply shouldn't dare to think of it. You don't understand, I am afraid, the way we live down at Wellham Springs. We have really no servants, and we do everything ourselves. I couldn't attempt to manage a house like this."

He smiled at her kindly.

"Perhaps," he said, "you would find it less difficult than you think. There is a housekeeper already, who sees to all the practical part of it. She only needs to have some one to whom she can refer now and then. You would have nothing whatever to do with the managing of the servants, the commissariat, or anything of that sort. Yours would be purely social duties."

"I am afraid," she answered, "that I should know even less about them."

"Well," he said, "I have some good friends who will give you hints. You will find it very much easier than you imagine. You have only to be natural, acquire the art of listening, and wear pretty gowns, and you will find it a simple matter to become quite a popular person."

She nerved herself to ask him a question. He looked so kind and good-natured that it did not seem possible that he would resent it.

"Uncle," she said, "of course I am very glad to be here, and it all sounds very delightful. But what about—Stella?"

He leaned back in his chair. There was a pained look in his face. She was almost sorry that she had mentioned his daughter's name.

"Perhaps," he said, "it is as well that you should have asked me that question. I have always been an indulgent father, as I think you will find me an indulgent uncle. But there are certain things, certain offences I might say, for which I have no forgiveness. Stella deceived me. She made use of information, secret information which she acquired in this room, to benefit some man in whom she was interested. She used my secrets to enrich this person. She did this after I had warned her. I never warn twice."

"You mean that you sent her away?" she asked timidly.

"I mean that my doors are closed to her," he answered gravely, "as they would be closed upon you if you behaved as Stella has behaved. But, my dear child," he added, smiling kindly at her, "I do not expect this from you. I feel sure that what I have said will be sufficient. If you will stay with me a little time, and take my daughter's place, I think you will not find me very stern or very ungrateful. Now I am going to ring for Mrs. Perrin, my housekeeper, and she will show you your room. To-night you and I are going to dine quite alone, and we can talk again then. By the by, do you really mean that you have never been to New York before?"

"Never!" she answered. "I have been to Boston twice, never anywhere else."

He smiled.

"Well," he said, "the sooner you are introduced to some of its wonders, the better. We will dine out to-night, and I will take you to one of the famous restaurants. It will suit me better to be somewhere out of the way for an hour or two this evening. There is a panic in Chicago and Illinois—but there, you wouldn't understand that. Be ready at 8 o'clock."

"But uncle—" she began.

He waved his hand.

"I know what you are going to say—clothes. You will find some evening dresses in your room. I have had a collection of things sent round on approval, and you will probably be able to find one you can wear. Ah! here is Mrs. Perrin."

The door had opened, and a middle-aged lady in a stiff black silk gown had entered the room.

"Mrs. Perrin," he said, "this is my niece. She comes from the country. She knows nothing. Tell her everything that she ought to know. Help her with her clothes, and turn her out as well as you can to dine with me at Sherry's at eight o'clock."

A bell rang at his elbow, and one of the telephones began to tinkle. He picked up the receiver and waved them out of the room. Virginia followed her guide upstairs, feeling more and more with every step she took that she was indeed a wanderer in some new and enchanted land of the *Arabian Nights*.

CHAPTER II.
COUSIN STELLA

"Well," he said, smiling kindly at her over the bank of flowers which occupied the centre of the small round table at which they were dining, "what do you think of it all?"

Virginia shook her head.

"I cannot tell you," she said. "I haven't any words left. It is all so wonderful. You have never been to our home at Wellham Springs, or else you would understand."

He smiled.

"I think I can understand," he said, "what it is like. I, too, you know, was brought up at a farmhouse."

Her eyes smiled at him across the table.

"You should see my room," she said, "at home. It is just about as large as the cupboard in which I am supposed to keep my dresses here."

"I hope," he said, "that you will like where Mrs. Perrin has put you."

"Like!" she gasped. "I don't believe that I could have ever imagined anything like it. Do you know that I have a big bathroom of my own, with a marble floor, and a sitting-room so beautiful that I am afraid almost to look into it. I don't believe I'll ever be able to go to bed."

"In a week," he said indulgently, "you will become quite used to these things. In a month you would miss them terribly if you had to give them up."

Her face was suddenly grave. He looked across at her keenly.

"What are you thinking of?" he asked.

"I was thinking," she answered, after a moment's hesitation, "of Stella. I was wondering what it must be to her to have to give up all these beautiful things."

His expression hardened a little. The smile had passed from his lips.

"You never knew your cousin, I think?" he asked.

"Never," she admitted.

"Then I do not think," he said, "that you need waste your sympathy upon her. Tell me, do you see that young lady in a mauve-coloured dress and a large hat, sitting three tables to the left of us?"

She looked across and nodded.

"Of course I do," she answered. "How handsome she is, and what a strange-looking man she has with her! He looks very clever."

Her uncle smiled once more, but his face lacked its benevolent expression.

"The man is clever," he answered. "His name is Norris Vine, and he is a journalist, part owner of a newspaper, I believe. He is one of those foolish persons who imagine themselves altruists, and who are always trying to force their opinions upon other people. The young lady with him—is my daughter and your cousin."

Virginia's great eyes were opened wider than ever. Her lips parted, showing her wonderful teeth. The pink colour stained her cheeks.

"Do you mean that that is Stella?" she exclaimed.

Her uncle nodded, and paused for a moment to give an order to a passing *maître d'hôtel*.

"Yes!" he resumed, "that is Stella, and that is the man for whose sake she robbed me."

Virginia was still full of wonder.

"But you did not speak to her when she came in!" she said. "You nodded to the man, but took no notice of her!"

"I do not expect," he said quietly, "ever to speak to her again. I have been a kind father; I think that on the whole I am a good-natured man, but there are things which I do not forgive, and which I should forgive my own flesh and blood less even than I should a stranger."

The colour faded from her cheeks.

"It seems terrible," she murmured.

"As for the man," he continued, "he is my enemy, although it is only a matter of occasional chances which can make him in any way formidable. We speak because we are enemies. When you have had a little more experience, you will find that that is how the game is played here."

She was silent for several minutes. Her uncle turned his head, and immediately two *maîtres d'hôtel* and several waiters came rushing up. He gave a trivial order and dismissed them. Then he looked across at his niece, whose appetite seemed suddenly to have failed her.

"Tell me," he said, "what is the matter with you, Virginia?"

"I am a little afraid of you," she answered frankly. "I should be a little afraid of any one who could talk like that about his own child."

He smiled softly.

"You have the quality," he said, "which I admire most in your sex, and find most seldom. You are candid. You come from a little world where sentiment almost governs life. It is not so here. I am a kind man, I believe, but I am also just. My daughter deceived me, and for deceit I have no forgiveness. Do you still think me cruel, Virginia?"

"I am wondering," she answered frankly. "You see, I have read about you in the papers, and I was terribly frightened when mother told me that I was to come. Directly I saw you, you seemed quite a different person, and now again I am afraid."

"Ah!" he sighed, "that terrible Press of ours! They told you, I suppose, that I was hard, unscrupulous, unforgiving, a money-making machine, and all the rest of it. Do you think that I look like that, Virginia?"

"I am very sure that you do not," she answered.

"You will know me better, I hope, in a year or so's time," he said. "If you wish to please me, there are two things which you have to remember, and which I expect from you. One is absolute, implicit obedience, the other is absolute, unvarying truth. You will never, I think, have cause to complain of me, if you remember those two things."

"I will try," she murmured.

Her thoughts suddenly flitted back to the poor little home from which she had come with such high hopes. She thought of the excitement which had followed the coming of her uncle's letter; the hopes that her harassed, overworked father had built upon it; the sudden, almost trembling joy which had come into her mother's thin, faded face. Her first taste of luxury suddenly brought before her eyes, stripped bare of everything except its pitiful cruelty, that ceaseless struggle for life in which it seemed to her that all of them had been engaged, year after year. She shivered a little as she thought of them, shivered for fear she should fail now that the chance had come of some day being able to help them. Absolute obedience, absolute truth! If these two things were all, she could hold on, she was sure of it.

A messenger boy was brought in, and delivered a letter to her uncle. He read and destroyed it at once.

"There is no answer," he said.

The messenger protested.

"I am to wait, sir, until you give me one," he said. "The gentleman said it was most important. I was to find you anywhere, anyhow, and get an answer of some sort."

"How much," Mr. Phineas Duge asked, "were you to receive if you took back an answer?"

"The gentleman promised me a dollar, sir," the boy answered.

Mr. Duge put his hand into his pocket.

"Here are two dollars," he said. "Go away at once. There is no answer. There will not be one. You can tell Mr. Hamilton that I said so."

The boy departed. Her uncle looked across at Virginia and smiled. "That is how we have to buy immunity from small annoyances here," he said. "All the time it is the same thing—dollars, dollars, dollars! That messenger boy was clever to get in. When we leave this restaurant, you will find that there are at least half a dozen people waiting to speak to me. It will be telephoned to several places in the city that I am dining here to-night. From where I am sitting, I can see two reporters standing by the entrance. They are waiting for me."

She looked at him with interested eyes.

"But why?" she asked timidly.

"Oh! it is simply a matter," he said, "of the money-markets. I have been doing some things during the last few days which people don't quite understand. They don't know whether to follow me or stand away, and the Press doesn't know how to explain my actions; so you see I am watched. You heard what I said," he asked, somewhat abruptly, "about those two things, obedience and truth?"

"Yes!" she answered.

"They say," he resumed, "that a wise man trusts no one. I, on the other hand, do not believe this. There are times when one must trust. Your mother and your father were both as honest as people could be, whatever their other faults may have been. I like your face. I believe that you, too, are honest."

"Remember," she said, smiling, "that I have never been tempted."

"There could be no bidders for your faithfulness," he answered, "whom I could not outbid. I am going to trust you, Virginia. There are sometimes occasions when I do things, or am concerned in matters, which not even my secretaries have any idea of. You only, in the future, will know. I think, dear, that we shall get on very well together. I am not going to offer you a great deal of money, because you would not know what to do with it, but so long as you remain with me, and serve me in the way that I direct, I am going to do what I feel I ought to have done long ago for your people down at Wellham Springs."

Her face shone, and her beautiful eyes were more brilliant still with unshed tears.

"Uncle!" she murmured breathlessly.

He nodded.

"That will do," he said. "I only wanted you to understand. For the next week or two, all that you have to do is to get used to your position. The small services which I shall require of you will commence later on. Now try some of that ice. It has been prepared specially. How do you like our New York cooking?"

"It is all too marvellous," she declared.

Then there came a sudden interruption. She heard the rustle of a gown close to their table, and looking up found to her amazement that it was Stella who was standing there.

"So you are my cousin!" Stella said, "little Virginia! I only saw you once before, but I should have known you anywhere by your eyes. No! of course you don't remember me! You see I am six years older. I mustn't stop, because, as I dare say you know, I am not on speaking terms with my father, but I felt that I must just shake hands with you, and tell you that I remembered you."

"You are very kind," Virginia faltered.

Her uncle had risen to his feet, and was standing in an attitude of polite inattention, as though some perfect stranger had addressed the lady who was under his care. He appeared quite indifferent; in his daughter's voice there had not been the slightest trace of any sentiment. A careless word or two passed between him and the man Norris Vine, who was waiting for Stella. Then they passed out together, and Phineas Duge calmly resumed his chair. Virginia, who had expected to find him angry, was herself amazed.

"By the by," Mr. Duge said, as he lit a cigarette, "always remember what I told you about that man. Be especially on your guard if ever you are brought into contact with him. I happen to know that he registered a vow, a year ago, that before five years were past he would ruin me."

"I will remember," Virginia faltered.

CHAPTER III.
STORM CLOUDS

Mr. Phineas Duge, since the death of his wife, had closed his doors to all his friends, and entertained only on rare occasions a few of the men with whom he was connected in his many business enterprises. On the arrival of Virginia, however, he lifted his finger, and Society stormed at his doors. The great reception rooms were thrown open, the servants were provided with new liveries, an entertainment office was given carte blanche to engage the usual run of foreign singers and the best known mountebanks of the moment. Mrs. Trevor Harrison, the woman whom he had selected as chaperon for Virginia, more than once displayed some curiosity, when talking to her charge, as to this sudden change in the habits of a man whose lack of sociability had become almost proverbial.

"If it were not, my dear," she said one day to Virginia, when they were having tea together in her own more modest apartment, "that I firmly believe your uncle incapable of any affection for any one, we should all have to believe that he had lost his heart to you."

Virginia, who had heard other remarks of the same nature, looked puzzled.

"I cannot see," she exclaimed, "why every one speaks of my uncle as a heartless person. I do not think that I ever met any one more kind, and he looks it, too. I do not think that I ever saw any one with such a benevolent face."

Mrs. Trevor Harrison laughed softly as she rocked herself in her chair.

"Dear child," she said, "New York has known your uncle for twenty-five years, and suffered for him. These men who make great fortunes must make them at the expense of other people, and there are very many who have gone down to make Phineas Duge what he is."

"I cannot understand it," Virginia said.

"Your uncle," Mrs. Trevor Harrison continued, "has a will of iron, is absolutely self-centered; sentiment has never swayed him in the least. He has climbed up on the bodies of weaker men. But there, in America we blame no one for that. It is the strong man who lives, and the others must die. Only I cannot quite understand this new development. I have never known your uncle to do a purposeless thing."

"You say," Virginia remarked slowly, "that he has no heart. Why did he send for me, then? Since I have been here, he has paid off the mortgage which was making my father an old man, he has sent my brother to college, and has promised, so long as I am with him, to allow them so much money that they have no more anxiety at all. If you only knew what a change this has made in all our lives, you would understand that I do not like to hear you say that my uncle has no heart."

Mrs. Trevor Harrison stopped rocking her chair, and looked at the girl thoughtfully.

"Well," she said, "what you tell me sounds very strange. Still, I don't see what motive he could have had for doing all this."

"Why should you suspect a motive?" Virginia demanded.

"Because he is Phineas Duge," Mrs. Harrison said drily. "But there, my dear child, I mustn't say a word against your uncle. He has been nice enough to me because I have promised to look after you. Does he want me to marry you, I wonder? I don't think that it would be very difficult."

Virginia blushed, and moved uneasily in her chair.

"Please don't," she begged. "I do not wish to think of anything of the sort. My uncle says that presently I am to help him."

"To help him," Mrs. Trevor Harrison repeated thoughtfully.

Virginia nodded.

"Yes! I don't exactly know how, but that is what he said."

Her chaperon looked thoughtful for a moment. So there was a motive somewhere, then! But, after all, what concern was it of hers? She was an old friend of the Duge family, and Phineas Duge had made it very well worth her while to look after his niece.

They were interrupted by some callers. It was an informal "At Home" which Mrs. Harrison was giving in honour of her young charge. Soon the rooms were crowded with people, and Virginia, slim, elegant, perfectly gowned, looking like a picture, with her pale oval face and wonderful dark grey eyes, was the centre of a good deal of attention. And in the midst of it all a girl, whom as yet she had not noticed, touched her on the arm and drew her a little away. She started with surprise when she saw that it was Stella.

"Come, my dear cousin," Stella said, "I want to have a little talk with you. Won't you sit down with me here? I am sure you have been doing your duty admirably."

Virginia was a little shy. She was not quite sure whether she ought to talk to her cousin. Nevertheless, she obeyed the stronger personality.

"Of course I know," Stella said, spreading herself out on a sofa, and smiling in amusement at the other's slight embarrassment, "that I am in disgrace with my beloved parent, and that you are half afraid to talk to me. Still, you must remember that you owe me a little consideration, for you have taken my place, and turned me out into the cold world."

"You must not talk like that, please," Virginia said quietly. "You know very well that I have done nothing of the sort. When my uncle sent for me, I had no idea that you were not still living with him."

"I lived with him for three years," Stella said, "after I had come back from Europe. I call that a very wonderful record. I give you about three months."

"I don't know why you should say this," Virginia answered. "I find my uncle very easy to get on with so long as he is obeyed."

Stella smiled.

"Ah, well!" she said, "I don't want to dishearten you, only you seem rather a nice little thing, and I am afraid you don't quite understand the sort of man my father is. However, you'll find out, and until you do I should have as good a time as I could if I were you. How do you like New York?"

"How could I help liking it?" Virginia answered. "I came here from a little wooden farmhouse in a desolate part of the country. I did not know what luxury was. Here I have a maid, a suite of rooms, an automobile, and all manner of wonderful things, all of my own."

"Will you be willing," Stella asked calmly, "to pay the price when the time comes?"

Virginia looked at her wonderingly.

"The price?" she asked. "What do you mean?"

Stella laughed a little hardly.

"Little girl," she said, "you are very young. Let me tell you this. My father never did a kind action in his life for its own sake. He never befriended any one for any other motive than that some day or other he meant to exact some return for it. Your time hasn't come yet, but there will be something some day which will help you to understand."

Virginia sat upright in her seat. A very becoming touch of colour had stolen into her cheeks, and her eyes were bright.

"I like to talk to you, Stella," she said, "because you are my cousin, and none of these other people are even my friends yet, but I cannot listen to you if you talk like this of the man who has been so kind to me, especially," she added, "as he is your father and my uncle."

Stella leaned over and patted her hand patronizingly.

"Silly little girl!" she said. "Never mind, we shall be friends some day, I dare say. You daren't come and see me, I suppose?"

Virginia shook her head.

"Not without my uncle's permission," she said.

"Quite right," Stella agreed. "Don't run any risks. We shall come across one another now and then, especially since my father seems determined to throw open his doors once more to the usual mob. By the by, does he ever say anything about me?"

"Nothing," Virginia answered, "except that you deceived him. He has told me that."

"Any particulars?" Stella asked.

"I am not sure," Virginia said, "that I ought to repeat them."

Stella sat quite still for a moment, and a slight frown was on her forehead.

"He has told you, then, why he sent me away?" she asked.

"Yes!" Virginia answered.

Stella shrugged her shoulders and rose.

"Well," she said, "I mustn't monopolize you any longer, or I shall be in disgrace."

She walked away with a little nod, leaving behind her a faint but uncomfortable impression. Virginia, an hour or so later, thought it best to tell her uncle of this meeting. They were standing together in one of the reception rooms, waiting for some guests who were coming to dine, and were alone except for a couple of footmen, who were lighting a huge candelabrum of wax candles.

"Uncle," Virginia said, "I met Stella this afternoon, and she came and spoke to me."

He looked at her without change of countenance.

"Well?" he said.

"I thought I ought to tell you," Virginia continued. "I was not sure how you felt about it."

"I have no objection," he said, resting his hand for a moment upon her shoulder, "to your talking to her whenever you may happen to meet. Only remember one thing! She must not enter this house. You must never ask her here. You must never suffer her to come. You understand that?"

"I understand," Virginia answered.

"And this man Vine, Mr. Norris Vine, have you met him?" he asked.

Virginia shook her head.

"No!" she said, "I have never seen him since that night at the restaurant."

"The same thing," Phineas Duge said, "applies to him. Neither of them must cross the threshold of this house. It is a hard thing to say of one's own daughter, but those two are in league against me, if their combination is worth speaking of seriously."

Virginia looked hopelessly puzzled. Phineas Duge hesitated for a moment, and then continued—

"There are phases of our life here," he said, "which you could not hope to understand, even if you had been born in this city. But you can perhaps understand as much as this. In the higher regions of finance there is very much scheming and diplomacy required. One carries always secrets which must not be known, and one does things which it is necessary to conceal for the good of others, as well as for one's own benefit. I have been for some years engaged in operations whose success depends entirely upon the secrecy with which they are conducted. Naturally, there is an opposing side, there always must be. There are buyers and sellers. If one succeeds, the other must fail, so you can understand that one has enemies always."

"It sounds," she murmured, "almost romantic, like diplomacy or politics."

He smiled.

"The secret history of the lives and operations of some of us, who have made names in this country during the last few years," he said, "would make the modern romance seem stale. Even odd scraps of news or surmises are fought for by the Press. The journalists know well enough where to come for their sensation. Our guests at last, I believe. Don't forget what I have been saying to you, Virginia."

CHAPTER IV.
A MEETING OF GIANTS

Phineas Duge, if his manners preserved still that sense of restraint which seemed part of the man himself, still made an excellent host. He sat at the head of his table, a distinguished, almost handsome personality, his grey hair accurately parted, every detail of his toilette in exact accordance with the fashions of the moment, his eyes everywhere, his tongue seldom silent.

Virginia watched him more than once from her seat, in half-unwilling admiration. She was ashamed to admit that her personal enthusiasm for him had in any way abated, and yet she was becoming conscious of that absolute lack of any real cordiality, of any evidence of affection in his demeanour towards her and every one else with whom he was brought into contact. She knew very well what the world's account of him was, for in the old days they had read sketches of his career up in the little farmhouse amongst the mountains. They had read of his indomitable will, of his absolute heartlessness, the stern, persistent individuality which climbs and climbs, heedless of those who must fall by the way. Perhaps he was really like this. Perhaps her first impressions had been wrong. Then, with a sudden wave of shame, she remembered the joyous, affectionate letters which every post brought her from the home, which notwithstanding all her sufferings, she had loved so dearly. She looked down at the pearls which hung from her neck. She saw herself in her spotless muslin gown. She felt the touch of laces and silk, all the nameless effect of this environment of luxury thrilled in her blood. It was better, she decided, that she did not think of the future at all. It was better that she should nurse the gratitude which she most assuredly felt.

The dinner-party that night consisted of men only, and although the conversation was fairly general, even Virginia had a suspicion that these men had not been brought together absolutely as ordinary guests for social purposes. Lightly though they all talked, there was something in the background. More than once the voices were lowered, allusions were made which she failed to understand, and half-doubting glances were thrown in her direction. One of these her uncle appeared to notice, and, leaning a little forward in his chair, he said a few words to the man at his side in such a way that they were obviously intended for the information of all.

"My niece," he said, "is going to take the part which I had once hoped my daughter might fill. If the occasion arises, you can speak of any matter of business in which we may be interested, before her. It is necessary," he continued, after a slight pause, "that there should be some one in my household who is above suspicion, I might almost say, above temptation. My niece will hold that post."

Then they all looked at her, and Virginia was a little frightened. It did not seem to her necessary, however, to say anything. Two of the men she met for the first time, but all were known to her by sight. There was Stephen Weiss, the head of a great trust, long, lean, with inscrutable face, and eyes hidden behind thick spectacles; Higgins, who virtually controlled a great railway system; Littleson and Bardsley, millionaires both, and politicians. It was a gathering of men of almost limitless power; men who, according to some of the papers, lived with their hands upon their country's throat. Littleson leaned over and spoke to her not unkindly.

"I am sure," he said, "that your uncle has made a wise choice. There are some secrets too great to be in one man's charge alone, and besides—"

Phineas Duge lifted his hand.

"Never mind the rest," he said. "I have not explained those circumstances as yet to my niece. If you are quite ready, we will take our coffee in the library." He turned to Virginia, who had risen at once to leave them. "In an hour and a half exactly, Virginia," he said, "come into the library. Not before."

She glanced at her watch and made a note of the hour. Then she wandered off to one of the smaller drawing-rooms, and, to relieve a certain strain of which she was somehow conscious, she played the piano softly. In the middle of a nocturne of Chopin's the door was opened, and a young man was shown into the room.

"I beg your pardon," he said, "you are Miss Longworth?"

She rose at once from the piano seat. He was not dressed for the evening, and he carried a felt hat in his hand. Nevertheless his bearing was pleasant enough, and he seemed to her a gentleman.

"I am Miss Longworth," she answered. "You want to see my uncle, I suppose? They have made a mistake in showing you in here."

"Not at all," he answered, with an ingratiating smile. "I know that your uncle is very busy, so I took the liberty of asking to see you. It is such a simple matter I required, that it was not worth while interrupting him. My name is Carr, and I am on the *World*. There was just an ordinary question or two I was going to put to your uncle, but you can answer them just as well if you will."

"You mean you are a reporter?" she asked.

"That's it," he assented. "Odd sort of life in a way, because it sends us round seeking sometimes for the most trivial information. For instance, your uncle had a dinner-party to-night, and I have stepped round for a list of the guests."

"I do not see," she answered slowly, "what possible concern that can be of your paper's."

He smiled indulgently.

"Ah, Miss Longworth!" he said, "you have just come from the country, I believe. You do not understand the way we do things in New York. Your uncle is a famous man, and the public who buy papers to-day are dead keen upon knowing even the most trifling things that such men do. In fact, I have been sent all the way up from down town simply to find out that simple matter. Of course, I could have asked the servants, but we always prefer to get our information from one of the family where possible. Now, let me see. Mr. Weiss was here, of course?"

Virginia hesitated, but only for a moment.

"If you really wish for these details," she said, "you must ask my uncle. I do not care to tell you."

"But say, isn't that rather rough upon your uncle?" he asked doubtfully. "We can't bother him with every little thing. Surely there can be nothing indiscreet in your giving me the names of your guests. Most people send them to the papers themselves."

"I do not know," Virginia said, "whether my uncle would wish me to do so. In any case, I shall do nothing without his consent."

The young man frowned slightly. This was not to be so easy as he thought.

"Well," he said, "I can get the names from your servants, without bothering your uncle. Must be rather interesting for you, Miss Longworth, to hear these famous men talk,"

She shook her head.

"I do not understand one half of what they say,"
she answered, "but what
I do understand doesn't sound in the least wonderful."

He smiled appreciatively.

"I can quite understand that," he said; "but there must have been some of the conversation that you understood. For instance, the Anti-Trust Bill that is coming before the House in a few weeks. They ought to have said some interesting things about that."

Virginia moved calmly across the room, and before the young man had perceived her intention she had rung the bell.

"I think," she said, "that you are a very impertinent person. Please go away at once."

He shrugged his shoulders as he turned towards the door. His expression was still entirely good-humoured.

"Don't be angry with me, Miss Longworth," he said, as he paused for a moment with his hand upon the knob of the door; "it's all in my day's work, you know. One has to try and find out these things, or one wouldn't be worth one's place. We had word down at the office that you had just come from the country, and that something might be done with you."

"And I think it was most unfair and ungentlemanly," Virginia began.

"It seems so, I dare say," he admitted, "from your point of view; but you must remember, Miss Longworth, that it is all part of a game which is played here all the time. Each side knows the other's moves; there is no deceit about it. Men like your uncle, who want to cover up their actions, take as much pains to hoodwink us, and use any means that occur to them to keep us in the dark when they want to. They just make use of us, and we have to try and make use of them. Good night, Miss Longworth!"

He left the room, and Virginia returned to the piano. Her fingers were shaking, however, and she was unable to play. She took up a book and tried to read. All the time she kept glancing at the clock. At last she rose to her feet and left the room. The hour and a half was up.

CHAPTER V.
TREACHERY

Somewhat to Virginia's surprise, when at last she stepped with beating heart into the library, she found her uncle alone. He was sitting in front of his open desk, a pile of papers before him, and a long, black-looking cigar between his teeth. Scarcely glancing up, he motioned her to a seat.

"In five minutes," he said, "I shall want to talk to you."

She sat down in one of the chairs, now vacant, which had been drawn up to the study table. The air of the room was heavy with tobacco smoke, and there were empty liqueur glasses upon the sideboard. Yet Virginia somehow felt that it was not only to take their after-dinner coffee, and enjoy a chat over their cigars, that these men had met together around the table before which she was sitting. She had the feeling somehow that things had been happening in that little room, of which she and Phineas Duge were now the only occupants.

"Virginia!"

She turned her head suddenly. Her uncle was looking at her. His eyes had lost their far-away gleam, and were fixed upon hers, cold and expressionless.

"Yes, uncle!" she said.

"I want to talk to you for a few moments," he said. "Listen, and don't interrupt."

She leaned a little toward him in an attitude of attention. The words seemed to frame themselves slowly upon his lips.

"You have been wondering, I suppose, like all the rest of the world," he began, "why I sent for you here. I am going to tell you. But first of all let me know this. Are you satisfied with what I have done for you, and for your people? In other words, have you any feeling of what people, I believe, call gratitude towards me?"

"I wonder that you can ask me that," she answered, a little tremulously. "You know that I am very, very grateful indeed."

"You like your life?" he asked. "You find it"—he hesitated for a moment—"more amusing than at Wellham Springs?"

"I am only an ordinary girl," she answered simply, "and you must realize what the difference means. Life there was a sort of struggle which led nowhere. Here I don't see how any one could be happier than I. Apart from that, what you have done for the others counts, I think, for more than anything with me."

"I am glad," he answered, "that you are satisfied. You think, perhaps, from what you have seen since you came here that the power of money has no limits. I can tell you that it has very fixed and definite limits, and it was when I realized them that I sent for you. I hope to gain from you what in all New York I should not know where to buy."

She was careful not to interrupt him, but her eyes were full of mute questions.

"I mean," he continued, "fidelity, absolute unswerving fidelity. The four men who have been here to-night call themselves my friends. We are leagued together in enterprises of immense importance. Yet take them one by one, and there is not one whom I can trust. I have proved it. I pay my two secretaries more highly than any other employer in the city. They do their duty, but I know very well that they only wait for some one else to outbid me, and they would take themselves and their knowledge of my affairs to whoever might call them. It has become necessary that there should be one person in whose charge I can repose the knowledge of certain things. New York does not hold such a person. That is why I have sent for you."

He paused so long that she ignored his injunction of silence.

"You know very well, uncle," she said, "that I am not clever, and that I understand nothing whatever about business, or anything to do with it, but I can at least promise that I will be faithful. That seems a very poor reward for all that you have done for me."

"Yes!" he answered, "I believe that you mean that. Now I must tell you this, that these four men who have dined with me here to-night, with myself, are under a solemn covenant to conduct all our operations upon the market and in finance, whether in this country or in Europe, absolutely in unison. We control practically an unlimited capital, and we pool all profits. We never speculate individually, at least that is a condition of our agreement. You may not understand this, but such a combination as ours, honestly adhered to, can do what it likes with the money-markets anywhere. We can bend them to our will. We buy or sell, and our profits are sure. We keep our agreement secret, but even then it is guessed at. I can assure you that we are probably the five best hated men in America. During the last two years we have made great fortunes. Our system is perfect. So far as the acquisition of wealth goes, there could be no object in any treachery, and yet one of these five men is playing a double game, if not more."

"You have found him out?" she asked breathlessly.

He shook his head.

"It is not so easy," he said, "only I know. To-night," he continued, lowering his voice almost to a whisper, "a new suspicion has come to me. I have an idea that there is a scheme, in which all four are concerned, for ruining me and sharing the plunder,"

"It is infamous!" she cried, turning pale.

He smiled slowly. It was the smile she hated. It seemed to change his face from the similitude of a benevolent divine to something hard, almost satanic.

"The odds," he continued, "seem heavy, but I have known one man hold his own against four before now. You may not understand all these different points, but I must tell you this. All through America, we millionaires, who operate largely upon the markets and control the finances of the country, are hated by the middle classes. We are hated by the merchants, the fairly well-off people, the labouring classes, and, more than any others, perhaps, by the politicians. Last month it was decided to strike a dangerous blow at us and our interests. A bill is to come before the Senate before very long which is framed purposely to undermine our power. Can you understand that?"

"I think so," she answered.

"It was to discuss this," he continued, "that we met to-night. I laid a trap for my four friends, and they fell into it. They have signed a document pledging themselves to resist this bill, in such a fashion that their doing so renders them parties to an illegal conspiracy. That document is in my possession. They all signed it, and it was left for me to be the last. No one noticed that my name was written across a piece of paper laid over the document itself. Now this I keep as a hostage over them. Sooner or later, when their plans mature, it will occur to them what they have done. They will remember that, so long as I hold this document, I have them in my power. Weiss was uneasy before he left the room to-night. In less than a week they will be trying to regain possession of that document under some pretext or other. I am going to show you where I keep it."

He pushed his chair away and pulled up the rug from beneath it. Even then Virginia, who had obeyed his gesture and was standing by his side, could see nothing unusual in the appearance of the hardwood floor. She watched his finger, however, count the cracks from a knot in the wood. Then he pressed a certain spot, and one of the blocks sprang up a little way and was easily removed. Beneath it was the steel lid of a small coffer, with two keyholes.

"This is my hiding-place," he said calmly, "and these," he added, "are the keys."

He laid before her two keys of curious device, and he took from a drawer in his desk a thin chain of platinum and gold.

"Now," he said, "you are going to be the guardian of these keys. You are going to wear this chain around your neck all the time, and the keys are going in here."

He drew from his pocket a gold locket, and touching the spring showed her that inside, instead of any place for a photograph, were little embedded pads of velvet, shaped for the keys. He placed them in and hung the locket around her neck. She looked at it, half terrified.

"I do not understand," she said, "why you trust me with this. Surely it would be safer with you!"

He smiled grimly.

"You do not know my friends," he said. "Remember that in my possession is not only the document which must cause them to abandon their great scheme of attack upon me, but also that that same document, if made proper use of, means ruin and ridicule for them. New York is a civilized city, it is true, but money can buy the assassin's pistol to-day as easily as it bought the bravo's knife a few hundred years ago. Have you ever thought of the number of unexplained, if not undetected crimes you read of continually, in which the victims are generally rich men? Perhaps not, and you need not worry your little head about it, but take my word for it, the keys are safer with you."

Virginia laid her hand tremulously upon the locket.

"They shall be safe," she said, "but tell me this. I am never to give them up to any one but you?"

"Never under any conditions," he answered.

"Not even," she asked, "if any one should bring a written message from you?"

"Distrust it," he answered. "Do not give them up. Into my hands only, remember that."

The telephone bell rang suddenly at his elbow. Phineas Duge took off the receiver and held it to his ear. The quiet, measured voice of Stephen Weiss came travelling along the wire.

"Say, Duge, I am half inclined to think we made a mistake in signing that paper," he said. "Of course, I know it's safe in your keeping, but I don't fancy my name standing written on a document that means quite what that means. I fancy that Higgins is a little nervous, too. We'll meet and talk it over to-morrow night."

Phineas Duge smiled faintly as he answered —

"Just as you like, only I must tell you that I entirely disagree. Unless we strike, and strike quickly, that bill will become law, and we shall all have to print a European address upon our notepaper, if we get as far."

"I speak for the others, too," Weiss continued. "We'll meet right here to-morrow night to discuss it. Say at eight o'clock."

Phineas Duge laid down the receiver and turned away.

"Well," he said, "this will become interesting. They will not strike now until they have got hold of that foolish paper. If they are all determined to get it back, and I resist, they will know that the game is up, and that I have seen through their little scheme. This must be thought about. Virginia, do I look ill?"

She shook her head.

"I thought you were looking very well, uncle," she said.

He locked up his desk, and looked down to see that the surface of the carpet was unruffled.

"To-morrow," he said, "I am going to be very ill indeed!"

CHAPTER VI.
MR. WEISS IN A HURRY

Virginia walked along Fifth Avenue, enjoying the sunshine, the crowds of people, and the effect of a new hat. Every now and then she stopped to look in a shop, and more than once she smiled to herself as she remembered how she had escaped from her uncle's house by flitting out of the side entrance. For she had found herself within the last few hours a very important person indeed. From the moment the doctor's carriage had stopped before the door, a little stream of callers, reporters, business friends, and others whom she knew nothing of, had thronged the place, unwilling to depart without some definite news of this unexpected illness, and all of them anxious to obtain a word or two with her. Already a "Special" was being sold on the streets, and in big black letters she read of the alarming illness of Phineas Duge. She had left both his secretaries, young men with whom as yet she had exchanged only a few words, hard at work opening letters and answering telegrams. She alone was free from all anxiety, for she had had a few words with her uncle before she came out, and at her entrance the languor of the sick man disappeared at once, and he had spoken to her with something of the enjoyment of a boy enjoying a huge joke.

She paused every now and then to look in the shop windows, and make a few purchases. Then, just as she was leaving a store, and hesitating for a moment which way to continue her walk, a man stopped suddenly before her and raised his hat. It was Stephen Weiss, gaunt, ill-dressed, easily recognizable. He was evidently glad to see her.

"This is real good fortune, Miss Longworth," he said, holding her hand in his, as though afraid that she might slip away. "I have just left your house, but I couldn't seem to get hold of anything very definite about this sudden attack of your uncle's."

"I know very little about it myself," Virginia answered. "The doctor had only just been when I came away. He said, I believe, that it was only a matter of a complete rest for several days, perhaps a week, and then possibly a short holiday."

Mr. Weiss shook his head thoughtfully.

"I am much relieved to hear that," he declared. "Your uncle is one of my oldest friends, and, apart from that, we are concerned in one or two very important speculations just now, things which you, young lady, would scarcely understand; but it would be awkward if he were laid up."

"The doctor thinks," Virginia remarked, "that he will be able to attend to anything very necessary in four or five days. They will not allow him, however, even to look at a newspaper until then."

Mr. Weiss nodded thoughtfully.

"You were going back toward the house, I see," he remarked. "Permit me to walk with you a little way."

Virginia hesitated for a moment.

"I have a little more shopping to do," she said. "I was not going home just yet."

Mr. Weiss, however, was already leading her across the street.

"My dear young lady," he said, "I have something very important to say to you. I am sure you will not mind going back to the house with me now and continuing your walk afterwards. It is in your uncle's interests as much as my own."

She allowed herself to be led along, and when they had reached the other side of the Avenue, Stephen Weiss, speaking earnestly, and stooping a little towards her, commenced his explanation.

"Your uncle," he said, "and three or four of us whom you met last night, are engaged just now in a very important undertaking. I cannot explain it to you, but it involves a great many millions of dollars, more than we could any of us afford to lose, although, as you know, we are none of us poor men. Now we can carry this thing right through without bothering your uncle, and make a success of it, but there is just one thing we must have, and that is a paper which he has locked away in his study, and which is a sort of key to the situation. I spoke to your uncle about it last night over the telephone, and he agreed to have it ready for me when I called this morning. I could not find any one at the house, however, who had received instructions about it, so I concluded that he had perhaps left word with you."

"No!" she answered, "he has not told me anything."

"Miss Longworth," he continued, laying his hand for a moment upon her arm, "you know from what your uncle said last night that we are all practically his partners. Now in his interests and all of ours, and naturally therefore in yours, we must have that paper. When we get home, just step into your uncle's room and say one sentence to him. Say that I am downstairs. He will know what I want, and I am sure he will tell you to give it to me. I hate to have to bother him just now, but I can assure you that it would do him a good deal more harm just when he is pulling round, to find that we were all on the wrong side of things, than to have just one sentence breathed into his ear now."

Virginia seemed to hesitate.

"The doctor's orders," she remarked, "were very strict. I am sure I don't know what to say."

"Doctors," Mr. Weiss said, "are all very well, but they do not know everything. Just those few words from you can do your uncle no possible harm, and they may save him a very bad relapse later on. I wouldn't press this thing, my dear young lady, if I wasn't convinced of its tremendous importance. You can trust me about that."

Virginia walked on for a few steps in silence. They were approaching her uncle's house, and already a small crowd of people were collected, reading the bulletin which was hung upon the railings. Mr. Weiss stopped short.

"Isn't there any way of getting in without being seen by all this crowd?" he asked. "They'll worry us to death with questions."

She nodded, and led him round the back way. Even here they were caught, however, by a reporter, whom Mr. Weiss brushed unceremoniously away. Virginia took her companion into a morning-room upon the ground floor, and motioned him to a chair.

"If you will wait here," she said, "I'll go upstairs and see my uncle. If I see that it is in any way possible, I will do as you ask."

"That's good," he declared. "If you don't mind, Miss Longworth, I'll just step into the study, where we were last night. I dare say one of your uncle's young men will be there, and there are a few minor details I'd like to talk over with young Smedley, if he's about."

"I will find Mr. Smedley for you," Virginia said, "when I come down. I am sure that he is not in the library, because my uncle uses that always as his private room. Please wait here until I come down."

She left him and made her way upstairs. The door of her uncle's bedroom was guarded by his man servant, who allowed her, however, to pass. Inside the room Phineas Duge was sitting in an easy-chair, carefully dressed, smoking a cigarette, and with a pile of newspapers by his side. On the table a few feet away was a telephone, the receiver of which he had just laid down.

"Well," he asked, looking up as she entered, "have they made a move yet?"

"I met Mr. Weiss on Fifth Avenue," she said. "He explained that you were all partners in some business undertaking of very great importance. Then he went on to say that they could carry it on all right without you, but that they must have one paper, which he said was the key to the position. He remarked that he had telephoned to you last night about it, and he is quite sure that you will give me orders to find it and give it up to him. He persuaded me even, you see, to break the doctor's orders."

Phineas Duge smiled quietly.

"I am too ill to be disturbed about such things," he said, lighting a fresh cigarette. "I do not know what paper he means. If you come and talk to me again about business matters, I shall send for the doctor. It is most unreasonable. By the by, where did you leave Mr. Weiss?"

"In the morning-room," she answered. "He wanted to go into the library, and he wanted to see Smedley, but I told him to wait where he was till I got down."

"I hope you will find him there," Phineas Duge said. "He can see Smedley if he wants to, on your responsibility of course. Those boys know nothing. Come up and tell me how he takes it."

Virginia went down to the morning-room and found it empty. She crossed the hall, opened the door of the outer library softly, and passed with swift silent footsteps into the smaller apartment. Mr. Weiss was standing there before her uncle's closed desk, regarding it contemplatively. He looked up quickly as she entered.

"Don't think I am taking a liberty, Miss Longworth," he said calmly. "This place has been a sort of office for us, and your uncle lets us do about as we please here. I trust you are going to unlock that desk and give me the paper I want."

Virginia shook her head slowly.

"I am sorry," she said, "but my uncle will not discuss business matters at all. He did not seem to remember anything about a paper, and he said that everything must wait until his head is a little clearer. I am sorry I disturbed him. I am afraid that the doctor will be very angry with me."

Mr. Weiss' face, clean-shaven and lined, with his spectacled eyes and thin, indrawn lips, was as expressionless as a face could be, but Virginia heard him draw a quick little breath, and his very attitude seemed to be the attitude of a man confronted with calamity.

"Miss Longworth," he said slowly, "this is very unfortunate."

"I am sorry," she answered.

"Will you sit down?" he said. "I have something to say to you."

She shook her head.

"I am afraid that I cannot stay now," she said. "I have so many things to do, and so many notes to write."

His spectacled eyes looked right into hers.

"This," he said quietly, "is important. There are times, Miss Longworth, when the junior in command of a great enterprise is faced with a crisis, when he or she is forced to act upon their own responsibility. The person who is great enough to rise to an occasion like this is the person who wins and deserves success in life. You follow me, Miss Longworth?"

"I suppose so," Virginia answered, a little doubtfully, although in her heart she understood him very well indeed.

"Miss Longworth," he said, "have you pluck enough to save us all several millions of dollars, and to make your uncle grateful to you for life? In other words, will you help me look for that paper?"

"Without my uncle's permission?" she asked.

"Without a permission which he would give you in one moment," Mr. Weiss declared, "if he was in a fit state to look after his own affairs.

Come, you shall not have to wait until he recovers. For a part of your reward, at any rate, there is a pearl necklace in Streeter's, which I saw yesterday marked forty thousand dollars. It shall be yours within half an hour of the time I get that paper, and I guarantee that your uncle will give you another like it when he knows what you have done."

Virginia shook her head sorrowfully. Her great eyes seemed full of real regret.

"Mr. Weiss," she said, "I am too dull and stupid to dare to do things on my own account. I can only obey, and I am afraid all these beautiful rewards are not for me. Even if my uncle sends me away when he gets well, I must do exactly as he told me, no more, nor any less, and one of those things," she added, turning and pressing the electric bell in the wall by her side, "was that no one, no one at all, should enter this room."

Mr. Weiss stood quite still. He seemed to be thinking, but Virginia could see that his hands were tightly clenched, and the bones of his long sinewy fingers were standing out, straining against the flesh.

"I am disappointed in you, Miss Longworth," he said. "You have a great opportunity. It need not be only a matter of the necklace—"

She held out her hands.

"You mustn't!" she begged. "I am too frightened of my uncle."

Then she turned suddenly and opened the door to the servant, whose approaching footsteps she had heard.

"Will you please show Mr. Weiss out?" she said. "He is in rather a hurry."

Mr. Weiss went without a word.

CHAPTER VII.
A PROFESSIONAL BURGLAR

There were three men in New York that day, who, although they occupied their accustomed table, the best in one of its most exclusive clubs, and although their luncheon was chosen with the usual care, were never really conscious of what they were eating. Weiss was one, John Bardsley another, and Higgins, the railway man, the third. They sat in a corner, from which their conversation could not be overheard; and as often before when their heads had been close together, people looked across at them, always with interest, often with some envy, and wondered.

"I'd like you both to understand," Weiss said, speaking with unaccustomed emphasis as he leaned across the table, "that I don't like the look of things. We tackled something pretty big when we tackled Phineas Duge, and if he has the least idea that these Chicago brokers have been operating on our behalf, it's my belief we shall find ourselves up against it."

Higgins, who was the optimist of the party, a small man, with the unlined, clear complexion and face of a boy, shrugged his shoulders a little doubtfully.

"That's all very well, Weiss," he said, "but if Phineas had been going to find us out at all, he'd have found us out three weeks ago, when the thing started. He wouldn't have sat still and let us sell ten million dollars' worth of stock without moving his little finger. I guess you've got the jumps, Weiss, all because we were d— —-d fools enough to sign that rotten paper last night. All the same I don't quite see how he could ever use that against us. His own name's there."

"I'm not so sure of that," Weiss said quietly. "I tell you it occurred to me to look across just as he was blotting the page, and I saw that he had his arm right round the paper, and it didn't seem to me that he was blotting the place where his signature ought to have been."

"Why didn't you ask to read the thing through again?" Higgins demanded.

"I wish I had," Weiss answered gloomily.

Bardsley, a large man, with grey beard and moustache, and coarse, hard face, spoke for the first time.

"Do any of you know," he asked, "whereabouts in that infernal little room of his Duge keeps his papers?"

Weiss looked up.

"I am not sure," he said. "I know that he has a small iron strong-box screwed into the inside of his roll-top desk, and of course there is a safe in the outer office; but I don't see how we're going to find out whether the paper we want is there."

"The girl seemed a fool," Higgins remarked. "Can't she be got at?"

"I have done my best," Weiss answered. "It strikes me she's just fool enough to stick to what she's been told, and she's too scared of her uncle to do more or less. She practically turned me out of his room this morning, when I was just having a look round."

"If there is really anything," Higgins said in a soft voice, "in what Weiss is hinting at, there's only one thing for us to do, and, difficult or easy, it's got to be done, even if we use our friends from down there."

He motioned with his head toward the window which was behind them, and which looked out over the river. They were all three silent for a moment. Then Weiss struck the table lightly with his clenched fist.

"Fools that we are!" he muttered—"babies! idiots! To think that such men as Bardsley and Higgins and myself are compelled to make use of criminals, to put ourselves practically in fear of the law, to get back a paper which we signed like babes in the wood. What if this illness of Duge's is a fake! Nowadays a man doesn't need to move from his room to do mischief in this world."

"I've been round to his broker's this morning," Higgins remarked. "He is doing nothing, has done nothing for weeks. He left off the day we all agreed to leave off."

"Why couldn't he be doing as we've done," Bardsley remarked, "and work from Chicago or Boston?"

Higgins grunted, and poured himself out a glass of wine.

"You fellows have got the nerves," he said contemptuously. "You're imagining things like a pack of frightened women. Duge can't swallow us up, even if he tumbled to our game. I don't believe there's anything in this funk of yours. As to signing that paper, well, we've got to run the Government of this country, as well as a good many other things, if the Government won't leave us alone. Duge's name is on it right enough, but if you fellows are really going to shake all day about it, let's have the paper, even if we blow up the house. I'll send for Danes to-night. We'll meet him down town somewhere—two of us, no more—and see what he can suggest. If we get that paper, and Duge's illness isn't a sham, he'll come downstairs to face the biggest smash that any man in New York has ever dreamed of, and serve him d——d well right. I'm sick of the fellow and his ways. For every million we've scooped, he's scooped two. Every deal we've been into, he's had a little the best of us. We are going to get our own back, but for Heaven's sake don't let us spoil the game because you fellows have got the shivers. We'll have another bottle of wine, and right after lunch I shall telephone down for Danes. Now let's chuck it. There's little Simpson and Henderson watching us like cats. They'll think we've got caught on something, or that we are going on the market. Eat your luncheon, and don't forget my supper-party to-night. The whole crowd from the Eden Theatre are coming. I only hope the reporters don't get hold of it."

* * * * *

A few hours later Virginia was summoned to her uncle's room. As she entered the door she passed a small, insignificant-looking man, plainly dressed, and of somewhat servile appearance, whom she remembered to have seen about the place several times since her arrival. He glanced at her in passing, and Virginia saw that his eyes, at any rate, were keen enough. She found her uncle, now fully dressed, walking up and down the room, with his hands behind his back.

"I have just had news of our friends, Virginia," he remarked. "They are evidently very much in earnest. If they can't get hold of that paper by strategy, they are going to try and steal it."

"Won't that be a little difficult?" she asked.

He smiled.

"More difficult than they imagine. The coffer itself is an inch thick, and the lock will stand anything but dynamite. However, I hear that they've engaged a professional burglar, so we ought to get some amusement out of it."

"How did you hear this?" she asked.

"The little man who has just gone out," he answered. "He is one of Pinkerton's detectives, or rather he was. He is in my service now, and spends most of his time watching these precious friends of mine. I expect they will make the attempt to-night."

"What are you going to do?" she asked. "Send for the police?"

Her uncle shook his head.

"Certainly not," he answered. "If it wasn't that I suppose they will arrange it so that the affair could not possibly be traced back to them, I should be in the room myself. As it is, I shall leave the matter to Leverson, the man who has just gone out. He will get as much help as he wants. Only if you hear a noise in the night, you will know what to expect."

Virginia shivered a little.

"There will be a fight, I suppose," she said.

"There may be some shooting," he answered. "In any case, I am not afraid of their opening my safe-box."

CHAPTER VIII.
FIREARMS

In the middle of the night Virginia was awakened by the sound of a revolver shot. She put on her dressing-gown, and, with an electric torch in her hand, started to descend the stairs. The house was already, however, a blaze of light. Electric alarm bells were ringing, and servants were hurrying toward the library. The man Leverson was sitting in an easy-chair, with an ugly gash across the temple, and one of his men had a revolver wound through the shoulder. One of the two burglars, however, whom they had surprised, was a prisoner in their hands, a pale, sullen-looking man, who had apparently accepted his fate quite philosophically. He was just being marched off by the uniformed police when Virginia arrived.

"Has anything been taken?" she asked Leverson.

"Not a thing, miss," the man answered. "There were three of them, but two escaped. One was Bill Danes, I'm sure o' that, and we can lay our hands upon him at any time. This one I don't know, but they meant business. They had enough dynamite with them to blow the house up."

She crossed to her uncle's desk and looked downward. The carpet had apparently not been disturbed. There were no signs that it had been touched at all.

"Are these men ordinary burglars?" she asked Leverson.

He hesitated.

"Why, I imagine so," he answered. "Their tools are as smart a lot as ever I saw in my life. They had spies all round the house to help them escape, and this one would have got away too, if I hadn't tripped him up."

"Curse you!" the bound man muttered.

Virginia looked at him and shivered.

"Well, I am glad you caught one of them," she said. "I will go and tell my uncle."

But Phineas Duge already knew all about it. He smiled when Virginia brought him her news.

"They must be desperate indeed," he said, "to run such risks. However, I suppose they have bought these fellows' silence safe enough."

The midday papers were full of the attempted burglary. Before the magistrates, the man who had been apprehended said not a word. He seemed to accept his position with stolid fatalism. The cross-examination as to his associates, and the motive of the attempted robbery, was absolutely futile.

Phineas Duge kept up during the day the assumption of severe indisposition. No one was allowed to see him. A bulletin posted outside announced that he had been ordered complete and entire rest; and all the time the telephone wires from his bedroom, high up in the back of the house, were busy flashing messages east and west, all over the country. The work in which he had been engaged was zealously pushed home. No one saw his secretaries coming and going so often from his room, and neither of them was willing to admit, in fact they flatly denied when questioned, that they had seen their chief at all. Towards afternoon, Virginia returned from a short drive in the park to be told that two gentlemen were waiting to see her. She found no one in the drawing-room or waiting-room, however, or any of the usual reception-rooms, and rang the bell for the butler.

"Where are these people, Groves," she asked, "who want to see me?"

"They are in the library, madam," the man answered.

"You mean in your master's room?" she asked, with a sudden presentiment.

"Yes, madam!" the man answered. "You see, they are Mr. Weiss and Mr. Higgins, two of the master's greatest friends, and they wished to see the room where the burglary took place."

Virginia looked at the man in cold anger.

"Groves," she said, "you had my orders that no one was to be admitted into that room."

"I am sorry if I did wrong, madam," the man answered. "I made exception in favour of these two gentlemen, because they were constant visitors here, and old friends of Mr. Duge's, and I scarcely thought that your orders would apply to them."

Virginia stepped past him and across the hall. She entered the room suddenly and closed the door behind her. Mr. Weiss, with a bunch of keys in his hand, was trying to find one that fitted her uncle's desk. Higgins, who held an open penknife, seemed to have been attempting to pry the lid. They started as they saw Virginia enter, and it flashed into her mind at once that they had waited to pay their visit until they had seen her go out, and that her return so quickly had disconcerted them.

"Mr. Weiss," she said, crossing the room towards them, "this room is in my charge. It is by my uncle's orders that no one enters it. I regret that you were shown here by a servant who misunderstood his instructions. Will you come into the morning-room with me at once?"

Mr. Weiss stood up. Higgins had moved a little toward the door, and Virginia suddenly realized that her retreat was cut off.

"Young lady," the former said, "you must forgive us both, and me especially, if we speak to you very plainly. I told you about the document in which we were interested, which your uncle was holding yesterday. We were willing to let it remain here under ordinary circumstances, but after the events of last night, we do not propose to let it stay here another hour. If your uncle is not well enough to be spoken to, then we must take the matter into our own hands. You can see for yourself what a risk we run, when only last night an attempt was very nearly successfully made to steal these papers,"

"I hear what you say," Virginia answered. "May I ask what you intend to do?"

"To break open this desk, if necessary," Mr. Weiss said, "and to find our way somehow or other into the interior of the coffer where these papers are."

"And supposing I tell you," she answered calmly, "that I shall not permit a second burglary in this room within twenty-four hours?"

Higgins came forward.

"Miss Virginia," he said, "pardon me, Miss Longworth, you look like a sensible young woman. I believe you are. Consider our position.

Our whole future as men of influence and character depends upon certain papers, of which your uncle had charge, being kept absolutely secret. We entrusted him with the care of them in health, but we are not prepared to let them stay here now that he is lying upstairs dangerously ill, and one attempt to steal them has already been made. Take the case at its worst; if your uncle should die, a seal would be put upon all his effects, and nothing in the world could stop those documents becoming public property. You can't realize what that would mean to us. It would mean ruin not only to ourselves, but to hundreds of others. It would mean a panic in all the money-markets of the world. We only meant that paper to remain in existence for a matter of twenty-four hours. We are fully determined that it shall not remain in this room any longer, guarded or unguarded. Can't you sympathize with us? Don't you see the position we are in?"

"Whatever is in this room," Virginia said, "is safe until my uncle is well enough to decide what shall be done. While he remains in his present condition I shall not allow anything to be disturbed."

"You have relations," Higgins said to her meaningly, "whom you would like to help. One could not offer to bribe you. Don't think that I mean anything of the sort. But between us we will give one hundred thousand dollars for those papers, and I guarantee that when your uncle recovers he will be quite willing to give you another hundred thousand for having been sensible enough to let us have them."

Virginia turned her back upon him.

"This is not a matter," she said, "if you please, Mr. Weiss, which I can discuss with you or your friend. I cannot let you stay in this room. If you will not go away, I must ring for the servants."

Higgins made a sudden movement, as though to seize her by the arms, but she was too quick for him. She wheeled suddenly round, and something very small but very deadly looking flashed out in her hand.

"You will force me," she said, "to treat you like thieves. I know that you are not, but I shall treat you as though you were if you don't leave this room. Don't think that this is a toy either," she continued. "Revolver shooting was one of our favourite recreations up in the country. Will you get up from that desk, Mr. Weiss?"

He stooped down and tried one of the keys from his bunch. Virginia did not hesitate. She pulled the trigger of her revolver, and a bullet whistled only a few inches from his head. He sprang upright in a minute.

"Damn the girl!" he said. "Higgins, take that thing away from her."

But Virginia was standing with her back to the wall, and Higgins, after one look into her face, shook his head.

"Don't be a fool, Weiss," he said. "This sort of thing won't do. You've lost your head. Beg Miss Longworth's pardon and come away. She is quite right. There is no excuse for our behaving like this."

Weiss hesitated for a moment, looked into Virginia's face himself, and with a shrug of the shoulders admitted defeat. The two men moved toward the door.

"I am going to call now upon your uncle's physician," Weiss said. "I am going to tell him that whatever the risk to your uncle may be, we must have an interview with him."

"As you please," Virginia answered. "That has nothing to do with me."

They left the room and closed the door behind them. Virginia, breathing a little quickly, crossed the room and tried the desk, but it was still fast locked. She looked down at the carpet and found it undisturbed. Then she stood up, and started violently. The inner door leading into the secretaries' room was open, and her uncle was standing there upon the threshold. He smiled at her benevolently.

"I congratulate you, Virginia," he said. "You have routed two of the worst scoundrels in New York. Now please help me to get upstairs again without being seen."

CHAPTER IX.
CONSPIRATORS

The great automobile swung out of the park into the avenue, and Stella drew a little sigh of regret.

"Mine is the next turning,"she said."

Thank you so much, Mr. Littleson.

I have enjoyed every minute of it."

Littleson smiled, but he did not slacken speed.

"I was very fortunate indeed to meet you," he said, "but I shall not think of letting you go until you have had some lunch. It is nearly one o'clock."

Stella settled down again in her seat.

"That is very kind of you," she said. "I had an idea that you were such a tremendously busy person, that you never stopped work for luncheon or trifles of that sort."

"A mistake, I can assure you," he said. "Which do you prefer, Sherry's or Delmonico's?"

"Martin's, if you don't mind," she answered. "I like watching a crowd of people."

They found a quiet table in one of the balconies, and Littleson devoted several minutes to ordering a luncheon which should be worthy of his reputation. Then he leaned across the table and looked steadily at his companion.

"Miss Duge," he said, "we have known one another for some time, although chance has never been very kind to me in the way of bringing us together. Now I am going to tell you something which I dare say will surprise you. When I saw you in the park this morning, I was on my way to call upon you."

She raised her eyebrows. She was certainly surprised.

"Do you mean that?" she asked.

"I mean it," he answered.

"But why? I have seen so little of you. I had no idea that you knew even what had become of me since I had left my father."

"I am going to explain everything by and by," he said, "but first of all I want to ask you one question. Do you know anything about this illness of your father's? Do you believe that it is a genuine thing, or that he has some motive of his own for keeping to his room?"

A faint smile parted Stella's lips.

"I begin to understand," she murmured. "I must admit that I was puzzled at your sudden interest in me."

"Does it need any particular reason?" he asked, looking at her admiringly.

Stella, who was conscious of a new hat and a very becoming gown, laughed softly.

"Well, perhaps it shouldn't," she said, "but, you see, you have given yourself away. But I may as well warn you at once that I know nothing about my father. He has even forbidden me the house, and I have not seen him for weeks,"

He nodded.

"So I understood," he said. "May I be quite frank?"

"Of course," she answered. "If you really have anything to say to me, I should prefer it."

"Then after the oysters I will undertake to be," he declared, smiling.

He turned away to send a boy out for some flowers and order some wine, and afterwards they proceeded with their lunch, talking of the slight things of the moment. Littleson, in that little group of millionaires, represented youth, and to a certain extent fashion. He came from one of the better-known families in New York. He had rooms and connections in London and Paris. He was fairly good looking, and always irreproachably dressed. Stella looked at him more than once approvingly. He was certainly a desirable companion. For the rest, she had little vanity, and she knew well enough that he had some purpose of his own in seeking her out. She had only known of him as one of her father's allies, and she was puzzled to know the meaning of that first question of his.

He seemed in no hurry, however, to satisfy her curiosity. He had ordered a wonderful lunch, and not until they had reached its final stage did he refer again to anything approaching serious conversation. Then he leaned a little across the table towards her, and she felt the change in his expression and tone, as he began to speak in lowered voice.

"Miss Duge," he said, "I dare say you were surprised at my question to you. Let me explain. Your father and several others of us have been allies for some time in some very important matters connected with finance. For the last few months, however, we have all felt a sort of vague uneasiness one with the other. Apparently we were all still pulling the same way, yet I think that each one of us had the feeling that there was something wrong. We all began to distrust one another. To come to an end quickly, I hope I do not offend you, Miss Duge, when I say that it is my belief that your father has been and is trying to deceive us for his own benefit."

Stella nodded assent.

"Well," she said, "I don't know why you should imagine that it could offend me to hear you say that. I understood that amongst you who control the money-markets there is no friendship, nor any right and wrong. At least if there is, it is the man who succeeds who is right, and the man who fails who is wrong."

"To a certain extent you are right, Miss Duge," he answered, "but you must remember that there is an old adage, 'Honour amongst thieves!'"

She shrugged her shoulders.

"Well," she said, "we won't discuss that. You have got so far in your story as to tell me that you believe my father is trying to get the best of you all, and you seem to be a little nervous about it. Well, I know my father, and I don't mind telling you that I should not be in the least surprised if you were right."

He lit a cigarette and passed the box across the table to her.

"Good!" he said. "It is a pleasure to talk to you, Miss Duge. You grasp everything so quickly. Now you understand the position, then. There are three or four of us, including myself, on one side, and your father on the other. Supposing it was in your power to help either, and your interests lay with us," he added, speaking with a certain meaning in his tone—"well, to cut it short, how should you feel about it?"

"You mean," she said slowly, "would my filial devotion outweigh—other considerations?"

He looked at her admiringly.

"You are a marvel, Miss Duge," he said. "That is exactly what I do mean."

She leaned back in her chair for a moment, and looked thoughtfully through the little cloud of cigarette smoke into the face of the man opposite to her.

"You have probably heard," she said, "that my father turned me out of his house."

"There was a rumour—" he began hesitatingly.

"Oh! it was no rumour," she interrupted. "He took care that every one knew that I had given Norris Vine some information about his doings in Canadian Pacifies. If I were back at home, which I never shall be, I would do the same thing again. I have lived with my father since I came back from Europe, and I know what manner of a man he is. I think," she continued, looking away from him, and speaking more thoughtfully, "that I was just like the average girl when I came back to New York. I lived with my father for two or three years, and—well—it would be a severe lesson for any one. However, this doesn't matter. And I am not over-sensitive. If you have anything to say to me, say it."

"I will," he answered. "We have an idea that at any moment there may be war between us and your father. I think that the odds would be very much in our favour but for one thing. Your father has a paper which we foolishly enough all signed one night, which places us practically in his power. If that paper were given to the Press, we should all of us be ruined men—I mean so far as prestige and position are concerned. Further, I am not sure that we should not have to leave the country altogether."

She looked at him in wonder. "Whatever made you sign such a paper?" she asked.

He shook his head.

"Heaven knows!" he answered. "We were a little mad. We did not mean to leave it in your father's charge, however. That is why this illness of his is so embarrassing to us. We can't help an idea that it is to keep out of our way for a few days, and to retain possession of that wretched document, that he is lying by. If, on the other hand, his illness is genuine, and he were, to put it bluntly, to die, that paper would be discovered by his lawyer, and Heaven knows what he would do with it!"

"I am beginning to understand," Stella said. "Now please tell me where I come in."

"We are willing," Littleson said quietly, "to give a hundred thousand dollars to the person who places that paper in our charge. To any one who knew your father's house, and where he keeps his important documents, the task would not be an impossible one."

She looked at him fixedly for several moments. He was half afraid that she was going to get up and leave him. Instead, however, she broke into a hard little laugh, and helped herself to another cigarette.

"You forget," she said, "that I have no longer the entrée to my father's house."

"It would be perfectly easy for you," he answered, "to go there, especially with your father out of the way upstairs. I presume that you know where he keeps his important papers?"

"Yes! I know that," she answered. "It is a pity," she added, with a faint smile upon her lips, "that those burglars didn't, isn't it?"

He shrugged his shoulders.

"A clumsy effort that, of course," he admitted, "especially when your father has a detective always round the place. He is well guarded, but I think that you could do better than that if you would, Miss Duge."

"About the paper?" she asked.

"It is simply," he answered, "a sheet of foolscap. I will not tell you exactly what is written upon it, but it contains a proposal with reference to raising a certain sum of money, to remove from office certain prominent politicians who are supporting this Anti-Trust Bill. Our names are all there, Bardsley's, Weiss', Seth Higgins', and my own. Your father's should have been there, but I believe he was too clever for us."

She began drawing on her gloves.

"Well," she said, "I have had a delightful morning, thanks to you, and these roses are lovely. Supposing I should feel that my gratitude still requires some expression, where could I write you?"

He handed her a card, which she tucked into her muff. They left the restaurant together, talking again of the people whom they passed, of the play at the theatre, of which they were reminded by the sight of a popular actress, and other indifferent matters. He offered his automobile, which she declined.

"I am going to make a call quite close to here," she said. "Good-bye!"

"I hope that I shall hear from you soon," he said, bowing over her hand.

"You may," she answered, smiling, as she turned away.

CHAPTER X.
MR. NORRIS VINE

Stella walked briskly down Fifth Avenue and turned into Broadway. Here she took a car down town, and presented herself in the space of twenty minutes or so before the offices of Mr. Norris Vine, at the top of a great flight of stairs in a building near Madison Square. Vine himself opened the door, and led her through the clerk's office into his own small but luxurious apartment.

"You were just going out?" she asked.

"It is no matter," he answered. "I have at least half an hour that I can spare."

He led her to his easy-chair, and seated himself in the chair before his desk. The sunshine fell upon his thin, somewhat hard face, and she looked at him thoughtfully.

"Are you getting older, Norris?" she asked, "or are things going the wrong way with you just now?"

He raised his eyebrows.

"It is a very strenuous life this," he remarked. "One has to crush all one's nervous instincts, and when one has succeeded in doing that, one finds oneself a little aged."

She nodded.

"You look like that," she said. "You look as though a good many of the fires had burned out, and left you—well, something of a machine. Is it worth while?"

"I don't know," he answered listlessly.

"You ought to go to Europe more often," she said softly. "I do not understand how men can make the slaves of themselves that you do here. Don't you long sometimes to feel your feet off the treadmill?"

"Perhaps," he answered; "but the life here becomes like one of those pernicious habits of cigarette smoking, or morphia taking. It grips hold of you—grips hold very tight," he added in a lower tone.

"I wonder," she said, "whether there is anything in the world which would tempt you to break away from it."

He struck the desk at which he was sitting, suddenly, with his clenched fist. His face was still colourless, but his black eyes held a touch of fire.

"Don't!" he said. "I am not such a slave, after all, as to love my chains; but don't you understand that one gets into this morass, and one can keep a foothold only by struggling."

"Is that how it is with you, Norris?" she asked.

"Yes!" he answered, with a sudden fierceness. "Six months ago I think that I might have freed myself. I shouldn't have been a rich man, but over there in Europe, where people have learned how to live, wealth isn't in the least necessary. I had enough for Italy, for a season in Paris, for a little sport in Hungary, even for a month or two at Melton. I hesitated, and while I hesitated the thing closed in upon me again. Then your father and I came up against one another once more, and I began it all over again."

"Am I right," she asked softly, "in imagining that just now things are going a little wrong?"

"I am fighting for my life," he said tersely. "Wherever I have turned during the last few months I seem to have encountered the opposition of your father's millions. Our sales are going down day by day. The great advertisers are practically ignoring us. We are losing money fast. That is what happens to any one who dares to raise a finger against the accursed idols of this country. Three of the greatest advertisement contractors have given us notice that they have struck off our paper from their list. It is your father's doings, Stella. I had hoped something from this illness of his, but the thing goes on. Do you know whether he is really laid up, or whether this is part of a scheme?"

"I am not sure," she answered. "I have been told to-day that it is part of a scheme."

"Who told you?" he asked quickly.

"Peter Littleson," she answered. "I have been lunching with him."

"Peter Littleson!" he interrupted. "But he is one of your father's allies! He and Bardsley and Weiss and your father are what they call here 'The Invincibles!'"

She nodded.

"I am not sure," she answered, "but I fancy there is going to be a split."

He was interested now, almost eager.

"Tell me what you know!" he begged.

"I know this," she answered; "that Littleson asked me to lunch to-day to find out whether my father's illness was genuine or not, and he gave me to understand that they suspected him of playing them false. I believe that as usual my father has the best of it. Peter Littleson admitted to me that just now, at any rate, he held them all in the hollow of his hand."

Norris Vine looked out of the window for a moment. His face was haggard.

"I have begun," he said slowly, "to lose faith in myself, and when one does that here the end is not far off. I believe that Littleson is right, Stella. I believe that your father, if it pleased him, could take them one by one and break them, as he is doing me."

"Supposing, on the other hand," she said, "something were to happen so that they were in a position to break him?"

"Then," he answered coolly, "it would be the very best thing that could happen for the country and for me. There's no morality about speculation, of course, and the finance of this country is one of the most ghastly things in the world. All the same, there are degrees of rascality, and there is no one who has sinned against every law of decency and respect for his fellows like Phineas Duge. What are you doing to-night, Stella? Will you dine with me?"

She shook her head.

"Not to-night, Norris," she said. "I have something else to do; but before I go I want you to answer me a question. Once before, when my father had you in a corner, I helped you out, and you know the price I paid."

He leaned toward her, but she waved him away.

"No!" she said, "I am not reminding you of that because I want anything from you, but listen. Supposing I could help you out again? Supposing I could give you something for your paper which would produce the greatest sensation which New York has ever known? Would you promise to realize at any loss, and give it up? Leave America altogether and go to Europe?"

"Yes!" he said, "I think I would promise that."

She rose to her feet. He approached her a little hesitatingly, but she waved him back.

"No, don't kiss me, Norris," she said.

He protested, but she still drew herself away.

"My dear Norris," she said, "please do not think because I show some interest in your affairs, that you are forced to offer me this sort of payment. There, don't say anything, because I don't want to be angry with you. If you knew more about women, you would know that there is nothing one resents so much in the world as affection that is offered in the way that you were offering me your kiss just then. Please come and put me in the elevator. I am going now. You will hear from me in a day or two. I shall write and ask myself to dinner."

He took her outside and rang the bell for the elevator. They stood for a moment in front of the steel gate.

"I am afraid," he said quietly, "that in your heart you must think me an ungrateful beast."

"Yes!" she answered, "I suppose I do! But then all men are ungrateful, and there are worse things even than ingratitude."

The lift shot up and the door was swung back. There was no time for any further adieux. Norris Vine walked slowly back into his office, with his hands clasped behind his back.

CHAPTER XI.
MR. LITTLESON, FLATTERER

Once more a little luncheon was in progress at the corner table in the millionaires' club. This time Littleson also was of the party. He had been describing his luncheon of the day before to his friends.

"I am dead sure of one thing," he declared. "She is on our side, and I honestly believe that she means getting that paper."

"But she hasn't even the entrée to the house now," Weiss objected.

"There are plenty of the servants there," Littleson answered, "whom she must know very well, and through whom she could get in, especially if Phineas is really up in his room. I tell you fellows, I truly believe we'll have that wretched document in our hands by this time to-morrow."

"The day I see it in ashes," Bardsley muttered, "I'll stand you fellows a magnum of Pommery '92."

"I wonder," Weiss remarked, "what sort of terms she is on with her cousin, the little girl with the big eyes."

"I wish to Heaven one of you could make friends with that child!" Bardsley exclaimed. "I'd give a tidy lot to know whether Phineas Duge lies there on his bed, or whether his hand is on the telephone half the time. You are sure, Littleson, that Dick Losting is in Europe?"

"Absolutely certain," Littleson answered.
"I had a letter from him dated
Paris only yesterday."

"Then who in God's name is shaking the Chicago markets like this!" Bardsley declared, striking the newspaper which lay by his side with the palm of his hand. "You notice, too, the stocks which are being hit are all ours, every one of them. Damn! If Phineas should be sitting up there in his room with that hideous little smile upon his lips, talking and talking across the wires hour after hour, while we hang round like idiots and play his game! It's maddening to think of."

"Oh, rot!" Littleson declared. "You can imagine everything if you try. There are the doctor's bulletins! We've had a dozen detectives all round the place, and there is not a single murmur of his having been seen by any one, or known to have even dictated a letter."

"I've never known him sick for a day in my life," Bardsley said thickly.

"It must come some time," Littleson answered. "It's always these men who've never been ill at all, who come down suddenly. I'm not going to worry myself about nothing. Our only mistake was in the way that child was handled. I think Weiss frightened her."

Weiss shrugged his shoulders.

"Perhaps I did," he said. "You see I'm not a fashionable young spark like you. Why the devil don't you go and call on her? It's only a civil thing to do. You are supposed to be one of her uncle's greatest friends, and he's supposed to be dangerously ill. Go and call on her this afternoon. Put on your best clothes and your Paris manners. You ought to be able to get something out of a child from the backwoods. If you talk to her cleverly you can at least find out whether Phineas is playing the game or not."

Littleson nodded.

"I'll call directly after lunch," he said. "Perhaps I could get her to come out for a ride. I'll try, anyhow, and ring you fellows up afterwards at the club."

"Don't bother her any more about the paper," Weiss said. "She'll get suspicious at once if you do. Try and make friends with her. This thing may drag on for a week or so."

Littleson nodded and left them soon afterwards. He went to his rooms, changed into calling attire, and before four o'clock his automobile was outside the mansion in Fifth Avenue, and he himself waiting in the drawing-room for Virginia. She came to him with very little delay, and welcomed him quite naturally.

"I am afraid," he said, "that you must look upon callers as rather a nuisance just now, but we are all very anxious about your uncle, and I thought I would like to hear something more than that little bulletin outside tells us."

She motioned him to sit down.

"You are very kind," she said. "My uncle is really about the same. The doctor thinks he may be able to get up in about a week."

"Is there any—specific disease?" he asked, hesitatingly.

"I think not," she answered. "I don't understand all that the doctor says. It seems to me that all you men here lead such strenuous lives that you have no time to be ill. You simply wait until you collapse."

"I'm afraid that's true, Miss Longworth," he said, "and if you will forgive my saying so, I fancy you have been doing a little too much yourself, worrying and looking after your uncle. Can't I tempt you out for a little way in my automobile? It's a delightful afternoon."

She shook her head.

"You are very kind," she said, "but I seem to be the only person for whom my uncle asks sometimes, and he is awake just now. I should not like to be away."

"He is conscious, then?" Littleson asked.

"Perfectly," she answered.

"I suppose it is quite useless asking to see him?"

"Quite. The doctor would never allow it. He has to be kept absolutely quiet, and free from excitement,"

"I hope," he said, "that he did not hear anything of the attempted burglary the other night?"

Virginia smiled very faintly, and her dark eyes rested for a moment upon his.

"No!" she answered, "we kept that from him. You see nothing was really stolen. As a matter of fact there was so little in that room which could have been of any value to any one."

"Exactly!" he answered, feeling a little uncomfortable.

"There are so many lovely things all over the house," she continued, "that it has puzzled me very much why they should have chosen to try only to break open that desk in the library. It seems queer, doesn't it?"

"Perhaps it does," he admitted. "On the other hand, they might have thought that your uncle had bonds and papers worth a great deal more than any of the ordinary treasures they could collect."

"Well," she said, "they got nothing at all. Somehow, I don't fancy," she added, "that my uncle is the sort of man to keep valuable things where they could possibly be stolen."

He determined to be a little daring. He raised his eyebrows, and looked at her with a smile which was meant to be humorous.

"Fortunate for him that he doesn't," he answered, "for, frankly, if I knew where to find it, I should certainly steal that document that Mr. Weiss came and worried you about. We ought to have it. If it got into any one's hands except your uncle's, it would be the most serious thing that ever happened to any of us."

"I don't think," she said reassuringly, "that you need worry. My uncle does not part easily with things which he believes have value."

He laughed, not quite naturally.

"I see," he said, "that you are beginning to appreciate your uncle."

"One learns all manner of things," she answered, "very quickly here."

He looked at her with more attention than he had as yet bestowed upon her. She was very slim, but wonderfully elegant, and her clothes, though simple, were absolutely perfect. Her eyes certainly were marvellous. Her complexion had not altogether lost the duskiness which came from her outdoor life. Her hair was parted in the middle, after a fashion of her own, and coming rather low on the back of her head, gave her the appearance of being younger even than she was. Stella's beauty was perhaps the most pronounced, but this girl, he felt, was unique. He looked thoughtfully into her eyes. Her whole expression and manner were so delightfully simple and girlish, that he found it almost impossible to believe that she was playing a part.

They talked for a little while upon purely general subjects, the Opera, her new friends, the whole social life of the city, of which he was a somewhat prominent part. She talked easily and naturally, and he flattered himself that he was making a good impression. When at last he rose to take his leave, he made one more venture.

"I don't know," he said, "whether you get bothered by your uncle's business affairs at all while he is laid up, but I hope you will remember that if I can be of any service, I am practically one of his partners, and I understand all his affairs. You must please send for me if I can be of the slightest use to you."

She had apparently listened to him for the first part of his sentence with her usual air of polite interest. Suddenly, however, she started, and her attention wandered. She crossed quickly toward the bell and rang it.

"Thank you so much, Mr. Littleson," she said. "I won't forget what you have said. Do you mind excusing me? I fancy that I am wanted."

She left the room as the servant whom she had summoned arrived to show her visitor out. Was it her fancy, or had she indeed heard the soft ringing of the burglar alarm which she had had attached to the library door on the other side of the hall!

CHAPTER XII.
STELLA SUCCEEDS

Virginia crossed the hall with rapid footsteps, and entered the library. She realized at once that she had not been deceived, but she started back in surprise when she discovered who it was standing before the roll-top desk and regarding it contemplatively. Stella looked up, and the eyes of the two girls met. Stella nodded, apparently quite at her ease.

"How are you, cousin Virginia?" she said. "You see I have come back home to play the part of the repentant daughter."

Virginia was a little distressed. She closed the door behind her and came further into the room.

"Stella," she said, "I am very sorry, but while your father is ill he does not like any one to come into this room."

Stella seated herself in his chair.

"Quite right," she said. "I hope you will be careful to keep them out. He always has such a lot of secrets, and I know that he hates to have people prying round."

Virginia felt that she had never received a more embarrassing visitor.

"Would you mind, Stella," she said, "coming into the drawing-room with me? This room is supposed to be locked up. You knew the catch in the door, of course, or you could not have come in."

"Yes! I know the catch," Stella answered, "and, my dear child, you must forgive my saying so, but I have lived here for some years, and it is still home to me. You, on the other hand, have been here a few weeks. I know you don't mean anything unkind, but just because I have quarrelled a little with my father, you must not tell me which rooms I may enter, and which I may not. I am going to stay here for half an hour, and write some letters."

"You can write them in any other room in the house," Virginia declared, "but not here. It is impossible."

Stella smiled and shrugged her shoulders as she sat down.

"I am sorry," she said, "but this is where I mean to write them. You must remember that this house belongs to my father. You are here temporarily in my place. I have not bothered you very much, and it is a very simple thing that I ask. I want to make use of this room, to write a few letters here. After that I shall go away."

The troubled frown on Virginia's face grew deeper.

"My dear Stella," she said, "although nothing would please me better than to see your father and you friends again, you must know that he allows no one to enter these rooms when his secretary is away. In fact, as you know, the door was closed, and if you had not known the secret of the catch, you could not have entered."

"Well," Stella repeated carelessly, "since I am here, I am here. Please unlock this desk and give me some writing paper."

"I cannot unlock it," Virginia answered. "You must know that."

"But you have the keys," Stella interposed.

"If I have," Virginia declared, "it is because your father trusted me with them."

"Perhaps," Stella said, leaning a little forward in her chair, "you have also the keys of that wonderful little hiding place of his that he showed me one day."

"Perhaps I have," Virginia answered, "but if so, no other person in the world will ever know about it."

"You won't even open the desk for me, then?" Stella said.

"Certainly not," Virginia answered. "Your father's orders to me were quite explicit."

"You do not suppose," Stella asked, "that he meant to exclude his own daughter?"

"How can I tell?" Virginia answered. "I know nothing of the trouble there was between you two," she added more softly, "It is not my affair, although nothing would please me more than to see you friends again. If you will come into the drawing-room and wait, I will go upstairs and try and persuade him to see you."

Stella shook her head.

"It would be of no use," she said. "He is frightfully obstinate, and I shall never have a chance of making my peace with him again unless I can come upon him unexpectedly."

"Well," Virginia said, "he is not likely to be downstairs to-day, and, Stella, don't be angry with me, but I must really ask you to leave this room."

"Thank you," Stella answered coldly. "I am at home here, and I mean to stay so long as I choose. It is you who are the intruder. If you have any sense at all, you will go away and play with your dolls. You can't have left them very long, and I'm sure it is a more fitting amusement for you than ordering me about my father's house."

Virginia moved up and down the room. The tears were already in her eyes; she was utterly and completely perplexed.

"Stella," she said, "you know what sort of a man your father is. If he learns that you have been here in this room, he will never forgive me. He will send me home, and that would be hateful, for many, many reasons. Do please be reasonable, and come away with me now into one of the other rooms. I will do all that I can to bring you two together."

Stella seemed to have made up her mind to quarrel with her cousin. Her face was white and hard. She laughed a little scornfully before she answered.

"You bring us together!" she exclaimed. "Do you think that I don't understand you better than that? I know very well that you are much too pleased with your position here, and you are afraid that if my father forgave me and I came back, you would have to go home again. Don't think that I don't understand."

Virginia walked to the window, and stood there several moments looking out upon the avenue. Her eyes were quite dry now, and a spot of colour was burning in her cheeks. The injustice of her cousin's words had checked the tears, but they had also achieved their purpose. She turned slowly round.

"Very well, Stella," she said, "I will not interfere with you any more, but I am going to do exactly what is my duty. Will you leave this room or not?"

"When I am ready," Stella answered, "not before!"

Virginia crossed the room, meaning to ring the bell. Stella, springing quickly from her seat, caught her cousin up, and seizing her by the shoulders, turned her round. Then she calmly locked the door of the room in which they were, on the inside.

* * * * *

About an hour afterwards, the elder of Phineas Duge's secretaries, Robert Smedley, entered the bedroom at the top of the house with some precipitation, and turned a white face towards his master. Phineas Duge, fully dressed, was entering some figures in a small memorandum book on the table before him.

"Mr. Duge," the young man exclaimed, "forgive me for disturbing you, but I think that if you feel strong enough you ought to come downstairs into the library at once."

Phineas Duge did not hesitate. There was a light in his eyes which transformed his face. He knew as though by inspiration something of what had happened. He took the back stairs, and descending at a pace quite extraordinary for a sick man, he was inside the library in less than a minute. It was easy to see that Smedley's alarm had not been altogether ill-founded. A chair was overturned; Virginia was lying face downwards upon the floor in front of the desk. Phineas Duge dropped his cigarette, and fell on his knees by her side. Then he saw that her hands and feet were tied with an antimacassar torn into strips, and a rude sort of gag was in her mouth. She opened her eyes at his touch, and moaned slightly. In a moment or two he had released her from her bonds, and removed the handkerchief which had been tied into her mouth.

"Fetch some brandy," he told the young man, "and keep your mouth shut about this. You understand?"

"Sure, sir!"

The young man hurried away. Duge was still stooping down, with his arm around Virginia's waist. Gradually she began to recover herself. She looked all round the room, as though in search of some one. Her uncle asked her no questions. He saw that she was rapidly regaining consciousness, and he waited. Smedley returned with the brandy. Together they forced a little between her lips, and watched the colour coming back into her cheeks. Then Phineas Duge withdrew his arm and walked to the other side of the desk. On the floor were the broken fragments of Virginia's locket. The carpet had been torn up. The steel coffer, with the keys still in it, was there half open. He slid back the lid, and taking out a few of the topmost papers, ran them through his fingers. There was no doubt about it. The document was missing. He returned to the chair to which he had carried Virginia.

"Are you well enough now," he asked, "to tell me about this?"

She raised herself in her chair, and looked with fascinated eyes toward that spot in the carpet.

"Has anything gone?" she asked.

"Yes!" her uncle answered shortly. "I want to know how it was that any one got into this room, and who it was. Quickly, please!"

"I was in the drawing-room talking to Mr. Littleson," Virginia said, "when I heard the small alarm bell that I had had fitted on to the library door ring. I came in and found Stella here. She locked me in. She is very strong. I had no idea that she was so strong," Virginia murmured, half closing her eyes and fainting away.

He hurried to her side, and forced some more brandy between her lips. Then he laid her flat on the floor, and began to walk up and down.

"So this is Stella's work," he muttered to himself. "That accounts for the message I had yesterday, that she was seen driving with Littleson. What she did for that blackguard Vine, she has done for them!"

His face, no longer an amiable one, grew sterner as he walked backwards and forwards, his hands behind him, his eyes fixed upon the carpet. He had staked a good deal on his possession of this hold upon the men who had been his associates. The whole situation had to be readjusted in the altered light of events. The first impulse of the man, to act, seemed strangled almost at its birth by the absolute futility of any move he could possibly make. He had no idea where to find his daughter, with whom she was living, or how. Any publicity of any sort was of course out of the question. No wonder that his frown grew heavier as he realized more completely the helplessness of his position. He was a man unaccustomed to failure, whose career through life had been one smooth road of success and triumph. His touch seemed to have transformed the very dust heaps into gold, and the barren wastes into prosperous cities. The shadow of failure had never fallen across his path. Now that it had come he was bewildered. An ordinary reverse he could have met resolutely enough. This was something stupendous, something against which the ordinary weapons of his will were altogether powerless. Try as he might, he could not see his way ahead. He was too deeply involved for any one to gauge the position accurately. A knock at the door. Phineas Duge looked up, and paused for a moment in his restless walk. He opened it cautiously and let in young Smedley, a tall, broad-shouldered young man.

"Come in, Smedley," he said shortly. "I have been wanting you."

The young man looked straight across at Virginia, still stretched upon the floor, and he took a quick step in her direction.

"What did you find was the matter with Miss Longworth, sir?" he asked. "Is she ill?"

Duge glanced carelessly towards his niece.

"She's only a little faint," he said. "There's matter enough here without that."

"What is it, sir?" the young man demanded.

Phineas Duge looked at him for a moment in silence, while he decided how much to tell.

"You remember my daughter Stella?" he asked abruptly.

The young man looked serious.

"I remember Miss Duge quite well," he answered.

"She has been here this afternoon. This is her work," Duge said grimly. "We had some trouble before, you know, about that Canadian Pacific report. It was after that, that I was obliged to send her away altogether."

The young man looked swiftly around the room.

"Has she taken anything?" he began.

"Nothing of importance," Phineas Duge answered calmly, "but that doesn't alter the fact that she might have done so!"

CHAPTER XIII.
BEARDING THE LION

Early the next morning, Littleson's automobile dashed up to the door of Weiss' office. Without even waiting to be announced, its owner pushed his way through the clerk's office and entered the private room of his friend.

"Heard the news?" he demanded quickly.

"No! What is it?" Weiss asked.

"Phineas Duge is in the city. He was going into Harrigold's as I came out. I tried to speak to him, but he cut me dead. They say that he has sent for all his brokers, and is coming on this market heavily!"

"Then his illness was a fake after all," Weiss declared. "We can't stand this, though. I'll get on to his office. We must speak to him."

He gave some rapid instructions to a clerk whom he had summoned, then took a printed sheet of prices from a machine which ticked at his elbow.

"If it's war," he muttered, "we shall have to fight hard, but what I don't understand is why he wants to break with us."

The clerk re-entered the room.

"There is a young lady here," he said, "who wishes to speak to you, sir."

"Name?" Weiss demanded curtly.

"Miss Virginia Longworth," he answered.

Weiss and Littleson exchanged quick glances.

"Show her in at once," Weiss ordered. "What do you suppose this means?" he asked, turning to Littleson.

The young man had no time to reply. Almost immediately Virginia was ushered into the office. She was very pale, and there were dark lines under her eyes. Stephen Weiss rose at once, and

Littleson hastened to offer her a chair, but she took no notice. They could see that she was agitated, and she seemed to find some difficulty in commencing what she had to say.

"What can I have the pleasure of doing for you, Miss Longworth?" Weiss asked. "I hope that you have come to tell me—"

"I have come to tell you that you are both thieves!" she interrupted. "If you do not give me back that paper, I don't care what my uncle says, I shall go to the police station."

The men exchanged swift glances.

Littleson suddenly started. He drew
Weiss on one side.

"Stella has got it," he whispered, in a tone of triumph. "Get rid of this girl easily. That is what she must mean."

Weiss turned round and faced her.

"My dear Miss Longworth," he said, "a thief I would have been if I could have found the chance, and a thief I would have made of you if you would have stolen that paper for me, because I considered that it belonged to us, and we had a moral right to take it. But the fact remains that we have not got it. When I heard your name announced I hoped that you had brought it to us."

"You have not got it!" she repeated contemptuously.

"Upon my honour we have not!" Littleson declared.

"Perhaps," she said, turning to him, "you will deny that it was you who incited my cousin Stella to come and rob her own father?"

The two men exchanged swift glances. Littleson's surmise had been correct then. It was Stella who had succeeded where the others had failed!

"We know nothing of Miss Duge," Littleson said, "nor have we received the paper nor any news of it. If Miss Stella has stolen it, she has not brought it to us. That is all I can tell you."

Virginia read truth in their faces. She turned away.

"Oh, I do not understand!" she said. "Perhaps I have made a mistake. I will go."

She hurried outside to the automobile which was waiting, and drove to the address which Stella had given her. It was a kind of residential hotel, and a boy in the hall took her up in the lift to the floor on which Stella's rooms were. She knocked at the door. Stella herself opened it. She started back when she saw who her visitor was.

"You!" she exclaimed.

Virginia stepped into the room.

"Yes!" she answered. "What have you done with the paper that you stole from the safe?"

Stella closed the door and looked at her cousin thoughtfully. She had evidently been busy packing. Dresses and hats lay about on the bed, and in the next room the maid was busy emptying the cupboards. Stella closed the communicating door.

"Why have you come here?" she said to Virginia. "You don't suppose I ran risks like that, to possess myself of a thing which I meant to give up. Oh! you need not look as though you were going to spring at me. I have not got it here, I can assure you. I parted with it hours ago!"

"To whom?" Virginia demanded.

"My father will find out some day, perhaps," Stella answered. "I don't see that it's so much his affair. The men who have to pay for their folly are the men who deserve to pay. I see that my father was too cunning to write his name down with theirs."

"You mean," Virginia demanded, "that you have not given it to Mr. Littleson and his friends?"

"Not I!" Stella laughed, —"although they offered me one hundred thousand dollars for it."

Virginia sat down on the bed. She had not slept all night, and she had eaten no breakfast.

"Stella," she said, looking at her cousin with her big eyes full of tears, and her voice becoming unsteady, "you have done a very, very cruel thing. You have ruined my life. Your father had done so much for my people, and now he is going to stop it all and send me back to them. You can't imagine what it means to be thrown back into such poverty. It isn't for myself I mind; it is for their sakes."

"I don't see," Stella answered, "how my father can blame you."

Virginia shook her head sadly.

"Your father is one of those men," she said, "who judges only by results. He trusted me, and whether it was my fault or my misfortune,

I was a failure. Stella, does it mean so much to you, after all, that you should keep that paper? Why don't you bring it back and be reconciled to your father? I should be quite content to go away; anything so long as he gets it back. Don't you understand that after he has been so kind, I hate the feeling that I have been so abject a failure?"

Stella smiled a little bitterly.

"It is my turn," she said, "to tell you that you do not understand my father. He would never forgive me, nor do I want him to. If you think that I was the tool of these men Littleson and Weiss, you make a mistake. What I did, I did for the sake of the only man I have ever cared for. Never mind his name, never mind who he is. But if it makes my father any happier, you can tell him that his friends are no nearer safety now than they were when the paper was in his keeping."

Virginia looked around the room drearily.

"You are going away?" she said.

"I am going to Europe," Stella answered. "I hate America. I hate the whole atmosphere here. It is a vile, unnatural life. I am going to try and live somewhere where people are simpler, and where life is not made up of gambling and plotting and senseless luxuries. I am tired to death of it all!"

"You are going to be married?"

Stella turned away and hid her face.

"No!" she said, "I do not think so."

There was a short silence. Virginia rose to her feet.

"Well," she said, "I think you have been a little unkind to me, Stella. I could have reached the bell and stopped you, only I hated to seem rude in your father's house."

"I am sorry," Stella said simply. "You see I am like all those other poor fools who care for a man. I put him first, and everybody else nowhere. Don't be afraid that I shall not have to suffer for it. I dare say if you know me, or anything about me, in five years' time, you will feel that you have had your revenge. If you take my advice, little girl," she added, speaking more kindly, "you will go back to your farmhouse and take up your simpler life there. I do not fancy that you were made for cities, or the ways of cities. I lived in the country once, and I was a very different sort of person. Run away now. I can do nothing for you, so it is no use staying, but if ever you need help, the ordinary, commonplace sort of help, I mean, write to me to Baring's, either in London or Paris. I'll do what I can."

Virginia went out again into the street and drove back home. Mechanically she changed her clothes and dressed for dinner. At eight o'clock she descended, shivering. Her uncle was already in his place. He rose as she entered, gravely, and took his place again as she sank into hers. His face was like a mask. He said nothing, and the few remarks which he made during dinner-time were on purely ordinary topics. There was only a minute or two, after the dessert had been placed upon the table and the remaining man servant had gone out with a message, during which they were alone. Then Virginia summoned up her courage to speak of the matter which was like a nightmare in her thoughts.

"Uncle," she said, "I think you ought to know this. I went to Mr. Weiss' office. He did not know that the paper was not still in your keeping. I went to Stella, and she told me that she had not taken it for them. She told me that they had offered her one hundred thousand dollars for it, but she never had any idea of letting them have it."

If Phineas Duge was surprised, he showed no signs of it, only he looked steadily into his niece's face for a moment or two before he replied.

"Stella," he said coldly, "has taken her goods to a poor market. Norris Vine is on the brink of ruin. If I turn the screw to-morrow, he must come down."

He sipped his wine for a moment thoughtfully. Then a grim, hard smile parted his lips.

"No wonder," he said, "that my friends are still in something of a panic."

Virginia rose in her place. It seemed as though her appearance was woebegone enough to soften the heart of any man, but Phineas Duge looked into her face unmoved.

"Uncle," she said, "I am no longer any use to you. I think that I had better go home."

He took out his pocket-book, looked through its contents, and passed it across the table to her.

"As you will," he answered. "I have a great weakness which I am always ready to admit. I cannot bear the presence about me of people who have failed. You have become one of them, and I do not wish you to remain here. If," he added, speaking more slowly, and looking meditatively into the decanter by his side, "if you saw any chance by which, with the help of what you will find in that pocket-book, a little application, a little ingenuity, and a good deal of perseverance, you could undo some part of the mischief which your carelessness has caused, then, of course, I should lose that feeling concerning you, and your place here would be open for your return. It would probably, also, be to the advantage of your people if any such idea as this resulted in successful action on your part. There is enough in that pocket-book," he added, "to take you where you will, and to enable you to live as you will for the remainder of the year, and during that time your people also are provided for. I leave the matter in your hands."

He turned and left the room. Virginia stood at the end of the table, clasping the pocket-book in her hands, and watching his retreating figure. He opened and closed the door. She sank back into her place for a moment and covered her face with her hands. For a moment she forgot where she was. The perfume of the roses, with which the table was laden, had somehow reminded her of the little farmhouse with its humble garden, far up amongst the hills.

CHAPTER XIV.
STELLA PROVES OBSTINATE

Littleson reached the hotel where Stella lived just in time to find the hall full of her trunks, and Stella herself, in dark travelling clothes and heavily veiled, in the act of saying farewell to the manager. He came up to her eagerly.

"I seem to be just in time, Miss Duge," he said. "You are going away?"

"I am certainly going away," she answered. "Did you wish to see me?"

Her manner took him a little aback. Nevertheless he reflected that there were a good many people within hearing, and she was right to be cautious.

"Can I have three words with you?" he begged, "alone, anywhere?"

She led him into a sitting-room, which was fortunately empty.

"Well," she said, continuing to draw on her gloves, "what do you want, Mr. Littleson?"

"You know very well what I want," he answered quickly. "I have my cheque-book in my pocket, and I am ready to pay over the hundred thousand dollars. I know that you have the paper. If you like to wait for ten minutes, you can have the money in dollars."

"How do you know that I have the paper?" she asked calmly.

"Your cousin, Miss Virginia, has been to our office," he answered. "She thought, naturally, that you had brought it straight to us. I don't know whether she seriously expected that we would give it up again, but that seemed to be the object of her visit. At any rate, we learnt that you had succeeded."

Stella was busy with the last finger of her glove.

"Yes!" she said, "I succeeded. It was a brutal action, and I shall never quite forgive myself for it, but I got the paper."

"Well?" he said.

"Well?" she answered calmly.

A horrible misgiving came over him.

"You haven't parted with it?" he demanded anxiously. "You haven't let your father have it back again?"

"I have not parted with it," she answered, "to my father. On the other hand, I certainly have not got it. A hundred thousand dollars is a good deal of money, Mr. Littleson; but I did not commit theft for the benefit of you and your friends."

"What do you mean?" he asked hoarsely.

"Exactly what I say," she answered. "The paper is in safe keeping. You will probably hear before long who has it."

Littleson was speechless. All manner of horrible fears oppressed him. "You must tell me," he insisted hoarsely, "where it is, who has got it! This is infamous! Why, if I had not told you—"

"I should not have known anything about it," she interrupted. "Quite true! I suppose I ought to thank you. However, as I say, the paper is in safe hands, but not my father's. You will probably hear something about it before long."

"For God's sake, tell me who has it, Miss Duge!" he implored. "You can't understand what this means to us. We were fools to sign it, I know; but your father insisted, and we had, I suppose, a weak moment. After all, there isn't anything so very terrible about it. We have a right to protect ourselves, we of the Trusts, whether our cause be just or not."

"Exactly!" she admitted. "No doubt you will have a case. I hope you will find, supposing the worst happens, that popular sympathy will be on your side. Most things are bought and sold in this country. I don't quite know how the American public will appreciate this attempted buying of the conscience of her public men. It might perhaps make you temporarily a little unpopular, necessitate a trip to Europe perhaps, or something of that sort. Well, I wish you well out of it, and now I must really go. If you do have to come across in a hurry, Mr. Littleson, I may see something of you in Paris."

"You are going to Europe, then?" he asked breathlessly.

"By to-morrow morning's boat," she answered. "I am going to send my trunks down to the steamer, and stay with some friends to-night."

"At least," he begged, "come down and see Bardsley and Weiss. I'll take you down in the automobile. It shall not detain you five minutes."

She shook her head.

"I cannot see the faintest use," she answered, "in my going to visit your friends. I have really and absolutely parted with the paper, and the person in whose possession it is will no doubt communicate with you."

"His name?" Littleson demanded. "I must know his name."

"That," she answered, "I decline to tell you; but I dare say, if you hurry back to Mr. Weiss' office, you will find some news for you. Don't look so angry. We all have our own game to play, you know, Mr. Littleson. I dare say I have behaved a little shabbily to you, but, you see, I had myself to consider, and in New York you know what that means. *Au revoir!* I have an idea that I may see something of you in Europe."

She left Littleson, who went round to the bar of the hotel and had a big drink. Then he lit a cigarette and returned to his automobile.

"Well," he muttered, as he swung round toward the city, "I may as well go back and face the music...!"

Weiss' offices were crowded when Littleson returned. There was excitement upon 'Change, clerks were rushing about, telephones were ringing. Weiss himself, with his coat off, stood in the midst of it all, giving orders, answering the telephone, exchanging a few hurried words with numberless callers. He had a big unlit cigar in his mouth, which he was constantly chewing. He pushed Littleson into his private office, but he did not follow him for some time. When at last he came in, the uproar outside was declining. It was five o'clock, and business was over for the day. Weiss went to a small cupboard and took out a whisky bottle and some glasses. Before he spoke a word he had tossed off a drink.

"Big day?" Littleson asked, mechanically.

"The devil's own day!" Weiss groaned. "We are in it now thick, all of us, you and I, Higgins and Bardsley. Do you know that every minute of the time Phineas Duge was supposed to be lying on his back, he was buying on the Chicago market?"

"I am not surprised," Littleson answered. "It seems to me we ought to be able to hold our own, though."

"We may," Weiss answered, "but it's a big thing. Even if we come out safe, we shall come out losers. Well, did you see the girl?"

Littleson nodded.

"I saw her," he answered drily. "I fancy things are not moving our way particularly just now, Weiss."

"She has not the paper after all?" Weiss exclaimed.

"She has had it and parted with it," Littleson answered.

Weiss removed his unlit cigar from his mouth, and drew a little breath.

"You d— —d fool!" he said. "You bungled things, then?"

"I scarcely see where the bungling comes in," Littleson answered. "I offered her a hundred thousand dollars for that paper. She took the tip and got it somehow. How could I tell that she had another scheme in her mind?"

"One hundred thousand dollars!" Weiss muttered. "Better have offered her a million and made sure of it. We shall have to pay that now, I expect. Who's got it?"

"She would not tell me," Littleson answered.

Weiss felt his forehead. It was wringing wet. He went to the cupboard, poured out another drink, and lit his cigar.

"Did she give you any idea?" he asked.

"None at all!" Littleson answered. "Some one seems to have outbid us. I only know that it was not Phineas."

Weiss leaned back in his chair.

"It just shows," he said under his breath, "what fools the shrewdest of us can be sometimes. There were you and I, and Higgins and Bardsley, four men who have held our own, and more than held our own, in the innermost circle of this thieves' kitchen. And yet, when Phineas Duge sprung that thing upon us, and we saw the thunderbolt coming, we were like frightened sheep, glad to do anything he suggested, glad to sign our names even to that d — — d paper. Do you realize, Littleson, that we may have to leave the country?"

"If we do," he answered, "we are done for—I am at least. I am in Canadian Pacifics too deep. If I cannot keep the ball rolling here, I can never pull through."

"It all depends," Weiss said, "into whose hands that paper has gone. A week's grace is all I want, time enough to fight this thing out with Duge."

"Has he been near you?" Littleson asked. "Has he offered any explanation?"

Weiss shrugged his shoulders.

"None," he answered. "That little fool of a Leslie, the outside broker, must have given us away. I was afraid of him from the first. He was always Duge's man."

A clerk knocked at the door. He entered, bearing a card.

"Mr. Norris Vine wishes to see you, sir!" he announced.

Weiss and Littleson exchanged swift glances. The same thought flashed into both their minds. Neither spoke for fully a minute. Then Weiss, with the card crumpled up in his hand, turned to the clerk, and his voice sounded as though it came from a great distance.

"Show him in," he said.

Littleson sank into a chair. His eyes were still fixed upon his companion's.

"God in heaven!" he muttered.

CHAPTER XV.
THE WARNING

Norris Vine shook hands with neither of the two men he greeted upon entering the room. Weiss, now that he felt that a crisis of some sort was at hand, recovered altogether from the nervous excitement of the last few minutes. He bowed courteously, if a little coldly, to Vine, and motioning him to a chair, took his own place in the seat before his desk. His manner was composed, his face was set and stern. Behind his spectacles his eyes steadfastly watched the countenance of the man whose coming might mean so much. Littleson, taking his cue, did his best also to feign indifference. He leaned against a writing-table, close to where Vine was sitting, and taking out his case, carefully selected and lit a cigarette.

"Well, Mr. Vine," Weiss said, "what can we do for you? Are you too going to join in the hustle for wealth? Have you any commissions for us? You will forgive me if I ask you to come to the point quickly. Things are moving about here just now, and we have little time to ourselves. By the by, you know Littleson, I suppose? Your business with me is not so private that you object to his remaining?"

"Certainly not," Vine answered calmly. "As a matter of fact, my business concerns also Mr. Littleson. In fact, there are two other of your friends whom I should have been equally glad to have seen here."

"Indeed!" Weiss answered. "You mean?"

"Mr. Bardsley and Mr. Seth Higgins," Vine replied.

"No doubt," Weiss said, "Littleson and I will be able to convey to them anything you may have to say. Come to the point! What is it? Are you going to write another of your sledge-hammer articles, damning us all to hell? Perhaps you have come here for a little information as to our methods. We will do our best to help you. There are times when we fear enemies less than friends."

"I, certainly," Vine remarked, "do not come here as a friend, and yet," he added, "I am not sure that mine might not be called to some extent a visit of friendship. I have come here to warn you."

Weiss reached out his hand for a box of cigars, and biting the end off one, put it unlit into his mouth. He half offered the box to Vine, who, however, shook his head.

"Come," he said, "you are a little enigmatic. There is only one sort of business we understand here. People come to buy or to sell. Have you anything to sell?"

Norris Vine smiled quietly, as though at some thought which was passing through his brain. He raised his eyes to Weiss', and looked him steadily in the face.

"I am in possession," he said, "of something which I think, Mr. Weiss, you would give half your fortune to buy, but I have not come here to sell. I have come here to warn you of the instant use to which I propose to put a certain document, signed by you and Littleson, Bardsley and Seth Higgins. It seems that you have entered into a conspiracy to remove from their places in the Government of this country the men who are pledged to the fight against the Trusts which you control. By chance that document has come into my hands. I propose to let the people of America know what sort of men you are, who have become the virtual governors of the country."

Stephen Weiss' surprise was exceedingly well simulated.

"I presume, Mr. Vine," he said, "that you are not here to poke fun at us. Tell me, if you please, what document it is to which you refer."

"I think," Vine answered, "that I need not enter into too close details. It is a document which you and your friends signed at Phineas Duge's house, not many nights ago."

Weiss rose to his feet, crossed the office, and turned the key in the lock of the door. He was a big man, and his face was a little flushed. Littleson, too, had slid softly from the edge of the table, and was watching his friend's face as though for a signal. Norris Vine, long, angular, unathletic, showed not the slightest signs of discomposure. He was leaning back in his chair, gently twirling by its thin black ribbon the horn-rimmed eyeglass which he usually wore.

"Mr. Vine," Weiss said, "whatever attitude we may take up afterwards, there isn't the slightest need to play a part with you. We did sign that document, and we have been kicking ourselves ever since for doing so. It was Phineas Duge's idea, and we are fairly well convinced that he pressed us for our signatures as subscribers to the fund, simply for the purpose of having in his possession a document which might, if its contents were known, cause us some inconvenience. Am I right in assuming that he deceived us that night, that he himself never signed the paper?"

"His signature," Norris Vine answered, "certainly does not appear."

Weiss nodded.

"Just as I thought," he remarked. "There was every indication a few weeks ago of what has actually happened, namely a split between us and Phineas Duge. This document was the weapon with which he had hoped to obtain the master-hand over us. Now, instead of finding it in his hands, we find it in yours. What are you going to do about it?"

"I am going to use it," Vine answered. "I am going to use it to strike a blow against the abominable system of robbery and corruption which is ruining the finest of all God's countries."

"Very well," Weiss said, "I am not going to give away our defence, of course. We may treat the document as a forgery, concocted by you or by Phineas Duge, either of whom would have sufficient motives. We may insist upon it that it was an after-dinner joke. We may contest the meaning of the text, and swear that we intended to use none but legitimate methods in this fight. Or, to put the whole matter before you, we may use such powers as we possess to see that you are put out of harm's way before you have an opportunity to make use of that paper. You see we have alternatives. We are not absolutely without hope. Now I ask you this, as man to man. The value of that document is, after all, a matter of speculation to you. Put a price on it, and fight us with our own dollars."

Norris Vine shook his head gently.

"I think not," he said. "If you gave me half your fortunes, we should only come into the field level."

"We are not small men," Stephen Weiss said slowly. "We represent a great power, and a power for which we mean to fight. When I talk to you of money, I mean it. We will raise a million dollars for you before midday to-morrow, if you leave that paper in our hands."

"We may shorten this discussion," Norris Vine answered, "by my assuring you solemnly that neither one nor twenty million dollars would purchase from me this document. I have spent years, and every scrap of such ability as I possess, in writing against, and lecturing upon, and attacking in every way that occurred to me, your abominable methods for collecting into the hands of a few what should be the comfort and happiness of the many. I mean the wealth of this country. Not even at the peril of my life would I part with the most efficient weapon which has ever yet come into my hands."

"Then why, Mr. Vine," Littleson asked, bending over from his place, "have you come here to see us?"

"I have come," Vine answered, "because against you personally I bear no malice. I am not well acquainted with the laws of this country, but it seems to me that the verbatim publication of this paper would mean for you something more than financial ruin. It would probably mean the inside of a prison. Personally, I have not the least doubt that every one of you deserves to see the inside of a prison, but I am not vindictive. I give you your chance. If a trip to Europe in the *Kaiser Wilhelm* to-morrow morning seems to you opportune, you will certainly escape reading the record of your own folly in the evening papers."

Weiss threw away his half-chewed cigar, and taking another from the box, lit it deliberately.

"Now, Mr. Vine," he said, "you are a young man whose attention has never been turned to the practical affairs of life. You are a literary person, and you walk a good deal with your head in the clouds. You haven't the hard common sense of us business men to be able to determine exactly what the result in a commonplace world is of any definite action. I can assure you that no prison in America could ever hold me and my friends, and that our risk is not in any way so serious as you imagine. But, leaving out the question of our personal safety or convenience, I want to put this to you. If you publish the contents of that document in the evening papers to-morrow, you will produce in America the greatest and most ruinous financial crisis that the country has ever known."

For the first time Vine's cold, immobile face showed some signs of interest. He abandoned his somewhat negligent attitude, and sat up with an attentive expression.

"What do you mean?" he asked.

Weiss struck the table in front of him with his open hand.

"Don't you know," he said, "that Bardsley, Littleson, Higgins, Phineas Duge, and myself, are the blood and the muscle of this country, so far as regards finance? Every one of the great railroad stocks is controlled by us. Prices are more or less what we make them. Three of the greatest industrial undertakings which the world has ever known, in which are invested hundreds of millions of honest American capital, are still controlled by us. If you publish that document, whatever the ultimate results may be, there will be the worst scare in the American money-market which the world has ever known. London and Paris were never so ill-prepared to come to the rescue, as a glance at the morning papers will show you. You will not find a city nor a village in this country, or a street, I almost was going to say a house, in New York, where there will not be a ruined man to curse you and your ill-considered action. The shrinkage in values in a few hours, of good and honest stocks, will come to twice as much as would pay for the Russo-Japanese war. I doubt whether this country would ever recover from the shock. That, Mr. Vine, is precisely what would happen if you adopt the methods of which you have just warned us."

Weiss ceased speaking and replaced the cigar in his mouth. Littleson, a few feet off, felt the perspiration breaking out upon his forehead. His breath was coming fast. The slow, crushing words of his partner had worked him into a state of excitement such as he had scarcely believed himself capable of. And Norris Vine, the imperturbable, was obviously impressed. Weiss had spoken almost as a man inspired. To treat his words lightly seemed impossible.

"You have given me something," Vine said slowly, "to think over. I should be very sorry, of course, to bring about such a state of things as you have spoken of. At the same time, I am not, as you say, a practical man. I cannot follow you in all you say. It seems to me that if this immense depreciation of funds really took place, especially in the case of undertakings of solid value, the pendulum would swing back to its place very soon. Values always assert themselves."

"And the people who would benefit," Weiss said, leaning forward, "are the foreigners who stepped in with their gold and bought for themselves a share in our country at half its value."

He stopped to answer for a moment an insistent ringing of the telephone from the outer office. As he laid the receiver down he turned to Vine.

"Look here," he said, "you doubt my statement. Outside in the office there is waiting to see me, upon a matter of business, a man who is as much my enemy as you are. I mean John Drayton, Governor of New York. Would you call him an honest man?"

"Absolutely!" Vine answered.

"Would you consider him a shrewd man?"

"Certainly," Vine assented.

"Then look here," Weiss said. "I am going to ask him to come into this office. I am going to treat this matter as an academic discussion, and I am going to ask him then what the result would be of such a step as you propose."

"Very well," Vine answered. "I pledge myself to nothing, but I should like to hear John Drayton's opinion."

CHAPTER XVI.
A TRUCE

Weiss unlocked and threw open the office door, and a moment later returned with a tall, grey-headed man, with closely cropped beard and gold-rimmed eyeglasses. He shook hands with Vine warmly, and nodded to Littleson.

"What, you here in the lion's den, Vine?" he remarked, smiling. "Be careful or they will eat you up."

Vine smiled.

"I am not afraid," he said, "especially now that you are here to support me."

"Mr. Vine," Weiss said, "shows himself possessed of our natural quality, audacity. He is here, I frankly believe, to pick up damaging information against us, for use the next time he issues his thunders. We have been led into an interesting discussion, and we have a point to refer to you."

John Drayton sat down and accepted the cigar which Weiss passed him.

"Sure," he said, "I'll be very pleased to join in; but you are a rash man, Weiss, to refer to me, for you know very well my sympathies are with Mr. Vine here. I hate you millionaires and your Trusts, on principle of course, although I must admit that some of you are very good fellows, and smoke thundering good cigars," he added, taking his from his mouth for a moment and looking at it.

"I don't care," Weiss answered. "The point I want you to decide scarcely calls upon your sympathies so much as your judgment. We were imagining a case in which say half a dozen men, who held the position of myself and Phineas Duge and Littleson here, I think I might say the half-dozen most powerful men in America, were suddenly, without a moment's warning, to lose in the eyes of the whole of the public every scrap of character and stability, were to be threatened with absolute ruin, and a term of imprisonment for misdemeanour. What would be the effect upon this country for the next forty-eight hours or so?"

John Drayton removed his cigar from his mouth.

"The one reason," he said impressively, "why I hate your Trusts, why I loathe to see all the power of this country gathered together in the hands of a few men such as you have mentioned, is that, in the event of such a happening as you have put forth, the country would have to face a crisis that would mean ruin to hundreds of thousands of her innocent people." Then for the first time during this interview Weiss' full round lips receded in a smile. His spectacles could not hide the flash of triumph that leapt out. He turned to Vine.

"You hear?" he said simply.

"Yes, I hear!" Norris Vine answered.

"Of course," John Drayton continued, "I do not know how you drifted into a conversation such as this, but in my last article in the *North American Review*, which Mr. Vine here will probably remember, I took the case of even a single man controlling one of the huge mercantile Trusts in this country, and tried to show what would happen to the small investors in a perfectly sound undertaking should a collapse happen to a holder of shares to this excessive extent. It is a painful thing to have to confess, but there is no doubt that it exists. We Americans are a great commercial people, and the dollar fever runs a little too hotly in our blood. We stretch out our hands too far. Vine, I know, agrees with me."

"Yes," Vine answered, "I agree with you!"

He rose to his feet. John Drayton followed his example.

"My business is really concluded," he remarked. "I had to see your manager on behalf of a client of mine. Are you coming my way, Vine? I am going to the club."

"I will follow you in a few minutes," Vine answered.

John Drayton went out, and once more the three men were alone.

"You see, Mr. Vine," Weiss said slowly, "this isn't the country or the age for Don Quixotes. Fight against our Trusts and our monetary system with all your eloquence, if you will, but don't tamper with things you don't understand, or you may do harm where you meant to do good. Now what can we say to you about that document?"

"I am not prepared," Vine said, rising, "to come to any definite decision at this moment. Frankly, I want to use it so as to do you the greatest possible amount of harm. On the other hand, I never contemplated any such developments as you and John Drayton have suggested. I am going to think this matter over."

"We are open enemies," Weiss said, "and there is no reason why we should not respect one another as such. We ask you to abide by the ways of civilized warfare. Don't strike without a word, at any rate, of warning. It will be in the interests of others, as well as ourselves."

"Very well," Vine said. "I promise that."

He left the office without any further word, without shaking hands with either of the two men. Weiss sat down in his seat, and Littleson, who was trembling all over, came to his side.

"Stephen," he said, "you're a great man. Come right along out of this and go to Parker's and have a bottle. My nerves are all on the twitch."

Weiss rose and put on his hat. The two men left the office together, and climbed into Littleson's automobile.

* * * * *

Vine walked thoughtfully down to his club. Amongst the letters which the hall-porter handed to him was one from Stella. He tore it open and read it standing there.

"MY DEAR NORRIS," it began, —

"Events have been marching a little too rapidly for me lately, and I am going away. I cannot stand New York any longer. Fifth Avenue gives me the horrors, and I am afraid to open an American paper. Besides, there are other things, to which I need not allude, which make me think that it would perhaps be better for me to take a journey. You will see from where I am writing I am on board the *Kaiser Wilhelm*. Where I shall go to in Europe, or what I shall do, I am not sure. I am not sure either that it would interest you to know. You are very absorbed in your profession, and I do not think that the things outside it mean much to you. I suppose that is the usual fate of us women. We are always willing to give, and we make no bargains. Don't think that I am reproaching you, only I have made America an impossible place for me just now. I could not bear to see that poor little cousin of mine, with her big reproachful eyes. Nor if you fill your purpose, and the storm comes, do I care to feel that I am responsible for the trouble which must surely follow.

"Good-bye, Norris! I wish you every sort of good fortune, and if I dared I would say that I wish you a little more heart, a little more understanding, and a little more gratitude!

"STELLA."

He folded the letter up and placed it carefully in his coat pocket. Then he went off into the reading-room in search of John Drayton. Life did not seem to him so absolutely simple a thing now, as a few hours ago.

BOOK II

CHAPTER I.
MY NAME IS MILDMAY

"I am quite sure," Virginia protested, a little shyly, "that you will want it yourself before long."

The young man laughed pleasantly.

"I am going to run that risk, anyhow," he said. "Please let me wrap it round you properly, so."

He did not wait for her consent, but after all she was scarcely prepared to withhold it, for it was a very cold morning, and the young man who had been sitting on the next chair, with an unused rug by his side, was wearing a particularly heavy fur coat.

"I think," he said, "that it is quite plucky of you to stay up on deck a morning like this. I suppose your people are all below?"

She shook her head.

"My people," she said, "are a very long way away."

"Your maid, then," he suggested. "Useless creatures maids, at a time like this. They are nearly always seasick, especially the first day out."

Again she shook her head.

"I am travelling quite alone," she said.

He looked at her in astonishment.

"Alone!" he repeated. "Why, you seem to me much too young. Forgive me, please," he added, apologetically, "I did not mean to be impertinent. I suppose you are an American?"

"I am," she admitted.

"Ah! that explains everything," he remarked with a little gesture of relief. "You belong, then, to the most wonderful race on earth, to the only race who have dared to cross swords with Mrs. Grundy and disarm her."

"On the contrary," she declared, "Mrs. Grundy of New York is quite as formidable as Mrs. Grundy of London, only we don't invoke her quite so often. Still, I will admit that, strictly speaking, I ought not to be travelling alone. The circumstances are very exceptional."

"I hope," he said earnestly, "that you will give me the opportunity of looking after you some of the time. I am quite alone, too, and I know no one on board."

She let her eyes rest for a moment or two upon his face. He was very fair, young, certainly not more than seven or eight and twenty, and reasonably good-looking; but apart from these things, he had eyes which she liked, a voice which was indubitable, and manners which left no possible room for doubt as to his status. She bowed her head alittle gravely.

"You are very kind indeed," she said. "I have never crossed before, and I am quite sure that if you have the time to spare, you can be ever so useful to me."

He smiled reassuringly.

"That's settled then," he said. "I can assure you that I feel very much more interested in the voyage already. By the by, my name is Mildmay."

"And mine," she replied, after a moment's hesitation, "is Virginia Longworth."

"Virginia," he repeated with a smile. "I think that is one of the most delightful of your American names."

"You are English, aren't you?" she asked.

He nodded.

"I," he said, "am returning from my first visit to the States. I have been to stay with a cousin who has a ranch out West. We had ever such a good time."

She looked at his sunburnt skin, and smiled to herself.

"Did you stay in New York?" she asked.

"Only two days," he answered. "Somehow or other those big places are rather terrifying. I had no friends there, and I wandered about as though I were in a wilderness."

"What a pity!" she murmured. "Americans are so hospitable. Surely you could have found some friends if you had wished to!"

He smiled a little whimsically.

"Yes!" he said, "I dare say I could, but I hadn't the time to spare to look them up. Now tell me about your visit to England. Where are you going to stay? In the country or in London?"

"I am not sure," she answered, "but I think in London, at first at any rate."

"You have relations there, of course?" he asked.

"None," she answered.

"Friends, then?"

She turned her dark eyes upon him. He felt himself suddenly embarrassed.

"I am awfully sorry," he said. "I've no right to ask you all these questions. The fact is, I was only trying to make sure that I should be able to see something of you after we had landed."

She smiled.

"I am afraid," she said, "that that will be scarcely possible, but, if you don't mind, you mustn't ask me any questions about my journey. I will admit that it is rather a peculiar one, that I have no friends in England, that I made up my mind to come all of a sudden. My journey has an object, of course, but I cannot tell you what it is, and you must not ask me."

"Of course I will not," he answered, "but I shall talk to you again about this before we land. I mean to say that you must let me give you my card, and you will know, at any rate, that there is some one in England to whom you can send if you are in need of a friend."

She smiled at him delightfully.

"And I have always been told," she said,

"That Englishmen were so slow! Why, I have known you scarcely a quarter of an hour."

"But I have watched you," he answered, "for two days."

"Well," she declared, "I like impulsive people, so I dare say I'll ask you for the card before we land. Do you live in London?"

"I have a house there," he answered. "I am there for about two months in the year, and odd week-ends during the hunting season."

"Tell me about London, please," she said.

"Historically," he began, a little doubtfully. "I am afraid—"

She interrupted him, shaking her head. "No!" she said, "tell me about the best restaurants and theatres, and how the people live." "That's a large order," he answered, "but I'll try."

They talked for an hour or more; neither, in fact, took an exact account of the time. Suddenly they looked up to see a dark-faced, correct-looking servant standing before them.

"The luncheon gong has gone, your Grace," he said. "Shall I take the rugs?"

They made their way into the saloon together. Virginia looked up at him curiously.

"You said that your name was Mildmay," she remarked. "What did your servant mean by calling you 'your Grace'?"

He laughed.

"Oh! I haven't had the fellow very long," he said, "and he came straight to me from some Italian duke, or nobleman of some sort. I suppose he hasn't got out of the habit yet. I wonder whether I can arrange to come and sit at your table. The purser seems rather a decent fellow."

"I haven't been in the saloon at all yet," Virginia said, "but it would be very nice if you could sit somewhere near me."

Mr. Mildmay found it an easy matter to arrange. His seat at the captain's table was exchanged for one at the purser's, and the two were side by side. Then Virginia, looking around, received a little shock. She heard her name spoken across the table, and, looking up, found that she was exactly opposite Mr. Littleson.

"How do you do, Miss Longworth?" he said. "I had no idea that we were to be fellow passengers."

She was almost too surprised to answer him coherently, but she faltered out something about an unexpected journey. Afterwards, on the way to her stateroom, she overtook him near one of the companion-ways, and laid her hand upon his arm.

"Mr. Littleson," she said, "would you do me a favour?"

"Why, I should say so," he answered. "Nothing I'd like better."

"Don't tell anybody anything about me," she begged, "I mean about my uncle, or anything of that sort at all. I am going over to England on a very foolish errand, I think, and I wish to keep it to myself."

Littleson became a trifle grave. He was not a bad sort of a fellow, and Virginia seemed little more than a charming child as she stood in the passage, looking up at him with appealing eyes and slightly parted lips.

"Do you mean," he asked, "that you have run away from your uncle?"

"Not exactly that," she answered. "My uncle was quite willing to have me leave him, but he does not know exactly where I am, nor do my people. Will you keep my secret, please?"

"Certainly!" he answered.

"Fromeveryoneonboard,aswellasfromyourlettersifyouwritefrom Queenstown?"

"Well, I'll try to do as you say," he answered, "but I should like to have a talk with you before we land."

He went to his stateroom a little thoughtfully. It had not yet occurred to him that Virginia's errand to London and his might possibly have something in common.

CHAPTER II.
REFLECTIONS

Littleson, before many hours of their voyage had passed, became conscious that Virginia was showing a slight but unmistakable desire to avoid his society. Being a Harvard graduate, something of an athlete, and a young man of fashion and popularity, he did not for a moment entertain the idea that there could be anything personal in her feeling. He came to the conclusion, therefore, that she had either discovered his connection with Stella's behaviour, or that the object of her visit to Europe was one that she desired to conceal from him. On the afternoon of the day when he had received his first but distinct snub, he made a point of drawing his chair over to hers.

"I am not going to bother you very much, Miss Longworth," he said, "but I feel that I must ask you a question. I don't want you to break any confidences, and I haven't much to tell you myself, but I should like to know whether your visit to England has anything to do with what happened one night in the library of your uncle's house?"

"So you know about that then, do you?" she asked quietly.

"I do," he answered. "I know that a paper was stolen by your cousin, and handed over to a person whom we will not name, but who is now in Europe. I will tell you this much—I am going across so as to keep in touch with that person. It seems odd that you, who are involved in the same affair, should be going over by the same steamer."

"The object of my journey," Virginia said, looking out seaward, "concerns nobody but myself."

The young man nodded.

"I expected that you would say that," he remarked coolly. "Still, our meeting like this induced me to ask you the question. If I can be of any service to you in London, I hope you will not fail to let me know.

Your uncle would never forgive me if I did not do everything I could in the way of looking after you."

Virginia smiled a little bitterly.

"My uncle," she said, "is not likely to trouble his head about me. He has dispensed with my services for the future. When I go home, I am going back to my own people."

Littleson was genuinely sorry. To a certain extent he felt that this was his fault.

"That's just like Phineas," he said. "Hard as nails, and without a dime's worth of consideration. I don't see how you could help what happened. You gave nothing up voluntarily. You told nobody anything."

"My uncle," Virginia said, "judges only by results. After all, it is the only infallible way. I am going to read a little now. Do you mind? Talking makes my head ache."

He bowed and went his way. For an hour or more he paced up and down on the other side of the deck, thinking. It was, of course, impossible that this child should have come across with the hope of wresting from Norris Vine the paper which all their offers and eloquence had failed to entice him to give up. And yet he did not understand her journey. He knew very well that Phineas Duge had neither connections nor relatives in England. Only a few weeks ago, in talking to Virginia at dinner-time, she had told him that she had no hope, at present at any rate, of visiting Europe. Later in the day he sent a marconigram back to New York. Perhaps Weiss would see something suggestive in the presence of this child upon the steamer!

* * * * *

"So you have found one friend on board," Mildmay remarked, pausing before her chair.

"He is not a friend," she answered, "and I do not like him. That is why I told him that it made my head ache to talk."

"Then I suppose—" he began.

"You are to suppose nothing, but to sit down," she said. "Talk to me about London, please, or anything, or any place. I am a little tired to-day. I suppose I should say really a little depressed. I cannot read, and I don't like my thoughts."

"You are such a child," he said softly, "to talk like that."

"I am nineteen," she answered, "and sometimes I feel thirty-nine."

"Nineteen!" he repeated, "and coming across to a strange country all by yourself. The American spirit is a wonderful thing."

She shook her head.

"It isn't the American spirit," she said simply. "It is necessity. I think that any girl, English or American, would prefer having some one to take care of her, to going about alone."

"You make one feel inclined—" he began, bending forward and looking into her eyes.

"After all," she interrupted, "I think I had better read."

"Please don't!" he begged, "I promise to talk most seriously. It is not my fault if I forgot for a moment. You looked at me, you know, and we are not used to eyes like that in England."

"You are either very silly," she said, "or very impertinent. I think that I shall send you away."

"There is no one else," he said, looking around, "to entertain you, and I am really going to try very hard to."

"Then please reach me up those chocolates and begin," she said. "Tell me about where you live in the country."

Mildmay, who had seven houses in different parts of the United Kingdom, was a little at a loss, but he talked to her about one, in which, by the by, he never lived, a gaunt grey stone building on the Northumbrian coast, whose windows were splashed with the spray of the North Sea, but whose gardens were famous throughout the north of England. He very soon succeeded in interesting her. She felt something absurdly restful in the sound of his strong, good-natured voice, with its slightly protective intonation. They sat there until the luncheon gong rang, and then they rose and walked for a time together. The sun had come out, and the grey sea was changing into blue. The decks were dry. The syren had ceased to blow. The motion of the ship had become soothing, and the spray, which leaped now into the air, sparkled in the sunlight like diamond drops.

"What a change!" she murmured, looking around.

"Wonderful, isn't it?" he assented. "And what a gloriously salt breeze!"

"I declare," she said, "I am positively hungry! I believe, after all, that I am going to enjoy this voyage."

After luncheon she hesitated for a moment, and then with a little sigh turned into her stateroom. She sat down upon her bunk, and leaning her elbow on the round space, gazed thoughtfully out of the open port-hole. Had she been foolish to forget for a little while, and was she in danger of being more foolish still! Her thoughts travelled back to the little farmhouse so far removed from civilization. She thought of the altered life they were all living there, her father freed from care, her brother at college, her mother with that anxious light banished from her eyes, no more having to scheme day by day how to pay the tradesmen's slender bills which so quickly became formidable. To think that the old days might return was a nightmare to her. She felt that she would do anything, dare anything, to win her way back to her old position with her uncle. Only a few words had passed between them at parting. She had asked him to let her people know nothing, to let them believe that she had gone on a journey for him.

"Let them have a few more months!" she begged. "Then if I succeed in what I am going to try, it will be all right. If I fail, well, they will have been happy for a little longer."

He had spoken no word of hope to her. He had made no promises. All that he had said had been curt and to the point.

"What you lost it is open for you to find. If it is found, it will be as though it were not lost."

But what a wild-goose chase it seemed! How could she hope for success! Even Stella would laugh at her; and Vine,—she had seen him only once, but she could imagine the smile with which he would greet any entreaties she could frame. She shook her head at her own thoughts. Entreaties! She would have to choose other weapons than these. By force and cunning she had been robbed; her only chance of effective reply would be to use the same means, only to use them more surely. Meanwhile she told herself that she must keep away from these distractions. After all, she was only a child, and she had had so little kindness from any one. Her head sank a little lower, and her hands went up before her eyes. What an idiot she was, after all! Then she locked the door, and cried herself to sleep.

CHAPTER III.
"WILL YOU MARRY ME?"

"This time," he said firmly, "you cannot escape me. Will you sit down in your chair, or shall we talk here?"

She glanced up at him, and the words which she had prepared died away on her lips. She led the way quite meekly to where their chairs remained side by side.

"We will sit down if you like, for a short time," she said, hesitatingly. "I cannot stay long. I still have a good deal of packing to do."

He did not answer until he had arranged her rug and made her comfortable. It was the last few hours of their voyage. Facing them they could see in the distance the lights of Wales. Next morning would see them in dock.

"I will not keep you very long," he said, drawing his chair quite close to hers, so that they could not be overheard, "but I insist upon knowing why for the last twenty-four hours you have done nothing but avoid me? I have not offended you in any way, have I?"

"No!" she answered, looking steadily away at the lights, "you know that you have not."

"On the contrary," he continued, "I have done what little I could to make the voyage more endurable to you. Of course I know the pleasure of your society more than compensated me for any little services I have been able to render, but still I have done nothing to deserve this altered treatment from you, and I am determined to know what it means."

"You are exaggerating trifles," she said coldly. "I have felt nervous and depressed all day, and I did not care to talk to any one. I have not avoided you more than anybody else."

"That," he answered, "is not true."

She turned slowly round till he could see her face, still and pale and cold, almost, it seemed to him, luminously white in the heavy darkness of the moonless hour.

"You can contradict me if you choose," she said, "but you can scarcely expect me to sit here and listen to you."

He leaned a little closer, and she suddenly felt her hand clasped in his.

"Virginia," he said,—"yes, I mean it—Virginia, don't be unkind to me, our last night. You know very well that it hurts me to have you speak and look at me so. Besides, we are going to be friends; you promised me that, you know."

"If I did," she answered, "it was very foolish. Friends means the giving and taking of confidences, and I have none to give. I am going to do strange things, and in an odd way, and I have no explanations to offer. If I had friends, they would think that I had taken leave of my senses, and they would want me to explain. That is just what I cannot do. That is why I am sure it would be better if you would let me alone."

"I shall not do that," he answered firmly. "I am not a morbidly curious person, nor do I want to pry into your affairs, but I cannot help feeling that you are in some sort of trouble, and that it would be good for you, in a strange country, to have some one on whose help you could rely in case of need."

"You mean well, I know," she answered, "but you are asking impossibilities. If you should happen to come across me over here, you will understand what I mean. I am going to do things which very likely you would be ashamed to think that any friend of yours would do."

He turned upon her a little angrily.

"Child," he said, "if I weren't so fond of you I think you would make me lose my temper. How old are you?"

"Nineteen," she answered, "but it isn't any business of yours."

"No business of mine!" he repeated. "Heavens! Isn't it the business of any man to look after a child like you? Nineteen years old, indeed, and most of them spent in a farmhouse! How do you know that these things which you talk about doing are right or necessary? Don't you see you are not old enough to be a judge of the serious things of life? You want some one to take care of you, Virginia. Will you marry me?"

"Will I what?" she gasped.

"Wasn't I explicit enough?" he asked. "I said marry me."

She would have risen from her chair, but he calmly took her arm and drew her down again.

"I will not stay here," she declared, "and hear you talk such rubbish."

"It is not rubbish," he answered, "but I will admit that I should not have said anything about it yet, if it had not been for your vague threats of what you were going to do. Virginia," he added, dropping his voice almost to a whisper, "you know that I am fond of you. I have been fond of you ever since I first saw you here."

"Six days ago," she murmured drearily.

"Six days or six weeks, it's all the same," he declared. "I wasn't going to say anything just yet, but I can't bear the thought of leaving you at Liverpool, in a strange country, and without any friends. Be sensible, dear, and tell me all about it later on. First of all, I want my answer."

"Is that necessary?" she replied quietly. "Even in America, we don't promise to marry people whom we have known but six days."

"Wait until you have known me longer, then," he answered, "but give me at least the chance of knowing you."

"You are a very foolish person," she said, a little more kindly. "You do not know who I am, or anything about me. Some day or other you will be very glad that I did not take advantage of your kindness."

"You think that I ask you this," he said, "because I am sorry for you?"

"I don't want to think about it at all," she answered, rising. "I am not going to sit here any longer. We will walk a while, if you like."

They paced together up and down the deck. She asked him questions about the lights, the landing at Liverpool, the train service to London, and she kept always very near to one of the other promenading couples. At last she stopped before the companion-way, and held out her hand.

"This must be our good night," she said, "and good-bye if I do not see anything of you in the morning. I suppose it will be a terrible crush getting on shore."

"It will not be good-bye," he said, "because however great the rush is I shall see you in the morning. As for the rest, you have been very unkind to me to-night, but I can wait. London is not a large place. I dare say we shall meet again."

The look in her eyes puzzled him no less than her words.

"Oh! I hope not," she said fervently. "I don't want to meet any one in London except one person. Good night, Mr. Mildmay!"

He turned away, and almost ran into the arms of Littleson, who had been watching them curiously.

"Come and have a drink," the latter said.

The two men made their way to the smoking room. Littleson lit a cigarette as he sipped his whisky and soda.

"Charming young lady, Miss Longworth," he remarked nonchalantly.

Mildmay agreed, but his acquiescence was stiff, and a little abrupt. He would have changed the subject, but Littleson was curious.

"Can't understand," he said, "what she's doing crossing over here alone. I saw her the first day out. She came and asked me, in fact, to forget that I had ever seen her before. Queer thing, very!"

Mildmay deliberately set down his glass.

"Do you mind," he said, "if we don't discuss it? I fancy that Miss Longworth has her own reasons for wishing not to be talked about, and in any case a smoking-room is scarcely the proper place to discuss her. I think I will go to bed, if you don't mind."

Littleson shrugged his shoulders as the Englishman disappeared.

"Touchy lot, these Britishers," he remarked.

CHAPTER IV.
THE AMERICAN AMBASSADOR

Conversation had begun to languish between the two men. Vine had answered all his host's inquiries about old friends and acquaintances on the other side, inquiries at first eager, then more spasmodic, until at last they were interspersed with brief periods of silence. And all the time Vine had said nothing as to the real object of his visit. Obviously he had come with something to say; almost as obviously he seemed to find a certain difficulty in approaching the subject. It was his host, after all, who paved the way.

"Tell me, Vine," he said, knocking the ash from his cigar, and leaning a little forward in his chair, "what has brought you to London just now. It was only a fortnight ago that I heard you were up to your neck in work, and had no hopes of leaving New York before the autumn."

Vine nodded.

"I thought so then," he said quietly. "The fact is, something has happened which brought me over here with one object, and one object only—to ask your advice."

The elder man nodded, and if he felt any surprise, successfully concealed it. Even then Vine still hesitated.

"It's a difficult matter," he said, "and a very important one. I have thought it out myself from every point of view, and I came to the conclusion that it would be better for me to come over to Europe for a week or two, and change my environment completely. Besides, I believe that you are the one man whom I can rely upon to give me sound and practical advice."

"It does not concern," the other asked, "my diplomatic position in any way?"

"Not in the least," Vine answered. "You see it is something like this. You know that since I became editor and part proprietor of the *Post* I have tried to take up a strong position with regard to our modern commercial methods."

"You mean," his host interrupted, "that you have taken sides against the Trusts?"

"Exactly!" Vine answered. "Of course, from a money-making point of view I know that it was a mistake. The paper scarcely pays its way now, and I seem to find enemies wherever I turn, and in whatever way I seek to develop it as a proprietor. However, we have held our own so far, although I don't mind telling you that we have been hard pushed. Well, a few days before I left New York there came into my hands, I won't say how, a most extraordinary document. Of course, you know within the last few months the Trusts have provoked an enmity far greater and more dangerous than mine."

His host nodded.

"I should say so," he answered. "I am told that you are going to see very exciting times over there."

"The first step," Vine continued, "has already been taken. There is a bill coming before the Senate very shortly, which, if it is passed into law, will strike at the very foundation of all these great corporations. Five of the men most likely to be affected met together one night, and four of them signed a document, guaranteeing a fund of one million dollars for the purpose of bribing certain members of the Senate, who had already been approached, and whose names are also upon the document. You must not ask me how or in what manner, but that document has come into my possession."

Vine's companion looked at him in astonishment.

"Are you sure of your facts, Vine?" he asked. "Are you sure that the thing is not a forgery?"

"Absolutely certain!" Vine answered.

"Then you know, of course," his host continued, "that you hold all these men in the hollow of your hand."

"Yes, I know it," Vine answered, "and so do they! They have offered me a million dollars already for the document, but I have declined to sell. While I considered what to do, I thought it better, for more reasons than one, that I did not remain in New York."

"I should say so," the other remarked softly. "This is a big thing, Vine. I could have scarcely realized it."

He rose to his feet, and took a few quick steps backwards and forwards. The two men were sitting in wicker chairs on a small flat space on the roof of the American Embassy in Ormonde Square. Vine's host, tall, with shrewd, kindly face, the stoop of a student, and the short uneven footsteps of a near-sighted man, was the ambassador himself. He had been more famous, perhaps, in his younger days, as Philip Deane, the man of letters, than as a diplomatist. His appointment to London had so far been a complete success. He had shown himself possessed of shrewd and far-reaching common sense, for which few save those who had known him well, like Norris Vine, had given him credit. He stood now with his back to Vine, looking down across the Square below, glittering with lights aflame with the busy night life of the great city. The jingle of hansom bells, and the distant roar of traffic down one of the great thoroughfares, was never out of their ears; but in this place, cut off from the house by the trap-door through which they had climbed, it was cooler by far than the smoking-room, which they had deserted half an hour before.

For some reason Deane seemed to wish to let the subject rest for a moment. He stood close to the little parapet, looking towards the horizon, watching the dull glare of lights, whose concentrated reflection was thrown upon a bank of heavy clouds.

"You have not told me, Norris," he remarked, "what you think of my attempted roof-garden."

"It is cool, at any rate," Norris Vine answered. "I wonder why one always feels the heat more in London than anywhere else in the world."

"It is because they have been so unaccustomed to it over here that they have made no preparations to cope with it," Deane answered. "Then think of the size of the place! What miles of pavements, and wildernesses of slate roofs, to attract the sun and keep out the fresh air. Vine, who are these men?" he asked, turning towards him abruptly.

Norris Vine smiled.

"Don't you think," he said, "that you can give me your advice better if you do not know? I can tell you this, at any rate. They are men who deserve whatever may happen to them. They are not of your world, my friend. They are the men who have sucked the life-blood out of many and many a prosperous town-village in our country. Don't think that I hesitate for one moment for their sakes. I tell you frankly that my first idea was to give the whole thing away in the *Post*."

"It would have been," Deane remarked, with a faint smile, "the biggest journalistic scoop of the century."

Vine nodded.

"Well," he said, "I should have done it but for one man's advice. It was John Drayton who showed me what the other side of the thing might be. He pointed out that the innocent would suffer for the guilty, in fact hundreds, perhaps thousands, of the innocent, would be ruined that these few men might be punished. It was his belief that the publication of this document, and the arrest of the men concerned in it, would cause the worst panic that had ever been known in America. That is why I stayed my hand and came over here to consult you."

The ambassador sighed, as he resumed his seat and lit another cigar.

"Drayton was right," he remarked softly. "He is a man of common sense, and yet we must remember that great reforms are never instituted without sacrifices. Could the country stand such a sacrifice as this? It is not a matter to be decided in a moment."

"There is no need for haste," Vine answered. "I have the document with me, and I do not mean to do anything in a hurry. Think it all over, Deane, and tell me when I may come and see you again."

"Whenever you will," the ambassador answered, heartily. "You know very well that I am always glad to see you. By the by, do you carry this document about with you?"

Vine shook his head.

"No!" he answered drily. "I have too much regard for my personal safety. The men whose names are there are fairly desperate, and they would not stick at a trifle to get rid of me."

"You are very wise," Deane answered.

"I should take care even over here.

I have heard of strange things happening in London. Oh, that reminds me.

A young lady was here only two days ago, asking for your address."

"Did she leave her name?" Vine asked, with a faint curiosity.

"I think not," the ambassador answered. "Wolfe saw her, and I asked him the question particularly."

"I cannot imagine whom she could have been," Vine said, thoughtfully. "I have not many acquaintances over here."

"Another man who was asking after you," Deane remarked, "was Littleson. He was dining here last night."

Vine smiled.

"I can imagine," he said, "his being curious as to my whereabouts. I have taken rooms where I don't think any one is likely to find me out except by accident."

Deane rose.

"I think," he said, "we had better go downstairs. The ladies will be wondering what has become of us. My wife is expecting a young woman in this evening whom I think you know—Stella Duge."

Vine started slightly.

"Yes," he said, "I have met Miss Duge often in New York."

CHAPTER V.
A QUESTION OF COURAGE

Stella turned towards him with a slight frown upon her forehead.

"Do you mean, Norris, then, that after all you will not use your power over these men, that you will let them go free?"

"Not if I can help it," he answered, "but there are many things to be considered. I shall be guided largely by what Deane advises."

"It is absurd," she declared. "You have wanted money all your life, money and power. You have both now in your grasp. If you do not use them, I shall think—"

She hesitated. He shrugged his shoulders slightly.

"Go on!" he said.

"I shall think that you are a coward," she said quietly. "I shall think that you are afraid to use what I risked—well, a great deal—to win for you."

"It isn't a question of courage," he protested.

"It is," she answered. "You are afraid to do what in your heart you must know is the right thing, because for a year or two, perhaps even a decade of years, it will mean a great upheaval. The end must be good. I am sure of it."

"If Deane and I," he answered, "can also convince ourselves of this, I shall act. You need not be afraid of that."

"Deane and you!" she repeated, contemptuously. "Who am I, then, in your counsels? Just a puppet, I suppose? Anyhow, it was I who ran the risk, I who gave these men into your hands. If you play the poltroon, everything is over between us, Norris."

He raised his eyes and looked at her in half-unwilling admiration. She and their hostess had come out on to the roof, just as the two men had been in the act of descending. A telephone call a few moments later had summoned Deane away, and his wife, who found the air a little chilly, had accompanied him. Stella was standing with her head thrown back, her figure tall and splendid in her evening gown of white satin, thrown into vivid relief against the background of empty air. She was angry, and the pose suited her. The slight hardness of her expression was lost in the dim blue twilight which still waited for the moon. Vine, an unemotional man, felt with a curious strength the charm of this isolation on the housetop, this tranquillity, so much more suggestive of solitude than anything which could be realized within the walls of a room. He shivered a little when he saw how close she was to the low parapet, and he held out his hand. She took it at once, and her face softened.

"Dear Norris," she said, "forgive me if I am disagreeable, but think what I went through to get that paper. Think how I have hoped that it might mean everything to you, perhaps to us."

She faltered, and it was in his mind then to speak the words which she had waited so long to hear from him, and yet he hesitated. He was a man who loved his freedom, not perhaps in the ordinary sense of the word, but he had still an almost passionate objection to lessening in any degree his individual hold upon life, to giving any one else a permanent right to share its struggles and its ambitions. He owed it to her, he was very sure of that, and yet he hesitated. She bent towards him. Perhaps she too felt that the moment was one not likely to be let go.

"Norris," she said, "don't listen to Deane or any of them. Strike your blow. Your paper will become famous. Trust to that for your reward if you will. If not a child, you could use your knowledge of what will happen on the morning of its appearance to make a fortune. Do you know I have grown to hate those men? If my father goes too, I do not care. I owe him very little, and I have had enough of luxury. There is more to be got out of a cottage in Italy or Switzerland, or even in England here, than a mansion in our country. I wish I could convert you."

He shrugged his shoulders.

"It is different with us," he said. "A man must be where life is. I do not think that I could ever be content with idleness."

"And yet when it comes," she reminded him, "you love it. Who was it who spent a year in some little village near the Carpathians, and had almost to be dragged back to civilization? Norris, sometimes I think that you are a *poseur*."

He looked down into the street. A carriage had driven up, and was waiting at the door below.

"We must go down," he said. "Mrs. Deane said ten minutes, and they are more than up. You see the carriage is waiting there to take you to the Opera."

She turned away reluctantly.

"Come with us," she begged, "or give us some supper afterwards. Mrs. Deane would like that."

"I'll meet you afterwards," he said. "I am not in the mood for music to-night."

"Very well," she answered. "If Mrs. Deane doesn't care about supper you can drive me home. Our talks always seem to be interrupted, and there is so much I want to say to you."

In the lobby of Covent Garden he met Littleson, who had paused to light a cigarette on his way out. He stepped forward and addressed Vine eagerly.

"I was trying to find you only this afternoon," he said. "Can you come around to the club with me now, and have a talk?"

"Sorry," Vine answered. "I am here to meet some friends who will be out directly."

"Will you lunch with me to-morrow?" Littleson asked.

"No!" Vine answered. "To tell you the truth, nothing would induce me to accept any hospitality at your hands."

"You have made up your mind, then?" Littleson asked slowly.

"Never mind about that," Vine answered. "I have said all that I have to say to you and your friends."

Littleson laid his hand for a moment upon the other's shoulder.

"Look here, Vine," he said, "you're what I call a crank of the first order, but you are not a bad chap, and I'd hate to see you make the mistake of your life. Weiss and the others are not the sort of men to take an attack such as you threaten, sitting down. You take my advice and leave it alone. Come round to my rooms, and we'll make a bargain of it. I can promise you that you'll never need to go back to America to make dollars."

"Life isn't all a matter of dollars," Vine answered contemptuously. "There are other things worth thinking about. If I strike at you and your friends, it is not for the money or the notoriety I could make out of it. It is because I want to attack a villainous system, because I consider that you and Weiss and the rest of you are really doing your best to throttle the greatest country on God's earth."

"Well," Littleson said, "I have warned you. You are a crank, and a foolish one at that. You are going about asking for trouble, and I think you will find it. If you change your mind, come to me at Claridge's."

He walked away, and Vine turned to greet Mrs. Deane and Stella, who were just coming out. Stella, whose eyes were still bright with the excitement of the music, laid her hand for a moment softly in his.

"Where are you taking us for supper?" she answered.

"To the Carlton, or anywhere you choose," he answered. "Let me find the carriage first."

Mrs. Deane held up her finger, and a tall footman, touching his hat, hurried away.

"James has seen us," she said. "The carriage will be here in a moment. I am going to speak to Lady Engelton. Will you look after Stella for a moment, Mr. Vine?"

She turned away to speak to a little group of people who were standing in one of the entrances. Stella and Vine stepped outside to escape the crush, and Stella suddenly seized his arm.

"Look in that hansom," she said, pointing out to the street.

Vine's eyes followed her finger. He recognized Littleson, and with him a man in morning clothes and low hat, a man whose face seemed familiar to him, but whom he failed to recognize.

"I think," she said, drawing a little closer to him, "that you must not hesitate any longer, if ever you mean to strike that blow. You saw Peter Littleson."

"Yes!" he answered, "I have been talking to him."

"Do you know who that was with him?"

Vine shook his head.

"I can't remember," he said.

"That is Dan Prince," she whispered. "You know who he is. They call him the most dangerous criminal unhanged. I should like to know what Littleson wants with him."

Vine smiled a little grimly, as he stepped forward to help Mrs. Deane into the carriage.

"I think," he murmured, "I can guess."

CHAPTER VI.
MR. MILDMAY AGAIN

It was her third day in London, and Virginia was discouraged. Neither at the Embassy nor at his club had she been able to obtain any tidings of the man of whom she was in search. There remained only a list of places given her in New York by his servant, where he was likely to be met. She went through them conscientiously, but without the slightest success. Gradually she began to realize the difficulty, perhaps the hopelessness, of her task. To find the man in London with such scanty information as she possessed was difficult enough, and there remained the question, as yet unanswered in her thoughts, as to what she would say or do if chance ever should bring them face to face.

Her experiences in those days became almost a nightmare to her. Dressed always in her quietest clothes, and with her natural reserve of manner intensified by the circumstances in which she found herself, she was yet more than once supremely uncomfortable. She became used to the doubtful looks of the waiters to whom she presented herself and asked for a table alone, at the different restaurants on her list. She found herself often at such times the only unescorted woman in the place, and the cynosure of a good many curious glances. Even when there were other women, they were of a class which she instinctively recognized, and from whom she shrank. But of actual adventures she had few. Apart from the fact of her appearing alone, there was nothing in her manner to invite attention.

There came a day, however, when she found herself suddenly plunged into the midst of more exciting events. She was sitting one afternoon in a café in Regent Street, at a table near the door, whence she could watch every one who came and went. Exactly behind her were two men, both strangers to her, who had been talking in low tones ever since her entrance. Her attention had been in no way attracted to them, and it was only by chance that she suddenly caught the name of Norris Vine.

Her heart gave a little beat. It was only by a strong exercise of will that she forbore to turn round. She pushed her chair a little further backwards, saying something to the waiter about a draught, and taking up a French newspaper which some one had left behind, she listened intently. All that she could remember of the men was that one was small, clean-shaven, very neatly dressed, and having rather the appearance of an American; and that the other was a larger and more florid man, with red face and burly shoulders. It was apparently the former who was speaking.

"It is a matter of five thousand pounds," she heard him say, "that is to say, two thousand five hundred pounds each, and it can be done without risk. The man is little known here, and has few friends. He has rooms in a flat to which there is plenty of access, two lifts on each floor and separate exits, and he lives quite alone."

"Two thousand five hundred pounds!" the other man uttered. "It sounds well, but—"

Then his voice dropped, and she could hear nothing else for a minute or two. She called a waiter and ordered something, she scarcely knew what. The voices behind had sunk lower and lower. She could hear nothing at all now, but she gathered that the smaller man was pressing some enterprise upon the other, and that his companion, although inclined to accept, found difficulties. She waited for a little time, and presently she began again to catch odd scraps of the conversation.

"Of course," she heard the smaller man say, "if we had him in New York the thing would be absolutely easy. It is probably because he knows that, that he came over here."

"He knows he is in danger, then?" the other voice asked.

"He knows that he carries his life in his hand," was the answer. "He must know that he has done so since a few days before he sailed for Europe. He is being watched the whole of the time, and from what I have seen, I should say his nerves were beginning to give way a little under the strain."

The other man muttered something which she could not hear.

"It is not your concern or mine," his companion answered. "He has chosen to court the enmity of some of the most powerful men in America, and it is his own fault if he suffers for it. He has been playing a pretty big game, but he doesn't hold quite all the cards."

There were more questions and answers, all unintelligible. She pushed her chair a little farther back, still apparently without awakening their suspicions, and then at last she heard something more definite.

"No. 57, Coniston Mansions. It is absolutely easy to get in. Nearly every one in the flats is connected with the stage, and they are almost deserted between half-past seven and eleven. To-night we know his movements exactly. He will dine at his club, and return some time before eleven to change, as he is going to a reception at the American Embassy."

"To-night is too soon," she heard the other man say. "I must have time to look about the place. I want to understand exactly where the risks are, and the easiest way to leave without being noticed. There are a lot of small things like that to be considered, if the matter is to be done artistically."

"Every day's delay is dangerous," the smaller man said, doubtfully. "Look here, Dick. It's a lot of money, and the offer may be withdrawn at any moment."

It occurred to Virginia suddenly that if these men were to see her face, she might be recognized. She could see that they were on the point of leaving, and their conversation was obviously at an end. She called for a waiter, paid her bill, and went out.

She walked slowly down Regent Street, and turning up Shaftesbury Avenue, made her way on foot to the boarding house near the British Museum where she was living. She went straight up to her room and sat down to think. She had decided that these men were probably employed by Littleson, and that they were going to make an attempt, that night apparently, upon the life of Norris Vine. In any case her first impulse would have been to warn him, but she had also personal reasons for doing so. If this paper which Vine held was recovered by some one else, her own mission would be a failure. In the hands of Littleson and his friends, it would without a doubt be promptly destroyed, and nothing would be left for her to do but to go back to America and own her defeat. She decided that Norris Vine must be warned. At first she thought of writing or telegraphing. Then she remembered that it was already past six, and that Vine was not expected to return to his rooms until after dinner. He would probably, therefore, receive neither telegram nor letter before he had walked into the trap. There was only one thing left for her to do. If these men could obtain ingress to Vine's rooms, so could she. She must be there first and warn him.

She changed her clothes, and after a few minutes' hesitation, set out to dine at one of the restaurants which she had on her list. It was a smart and somewhat Bohemian place, but even here women dining alone were subjected to a good deal of remark, and her cheeks grew hot as she remembered her first visit there, and the whispered discussion between the waiters as to whether she should be given a table. She had become a fairly regular customer there now, though, and to-night she was given a table near the wall, an excellent vantage ground for her, but exactly opposite three men, who had apparently been drinking heavily, and whose whole attention, from the moment of her entrance, seemed fixed upon her. She ordered her dinner, steadfastly ignoring them, and sat as usual with her eyes fixed upon the door, but her indifference was not sufficient to chill the ardour of the younger of the three men. She saw him call a waiter and write something on the back of a card, and immediately afterwards the waiter, with some hesitation, and a half-expressed apology, presented it to her. She tore it in pieces, and went on with her dinner without a word. Then a voice at her elbow startled her.

"Miss Longworth," it said, "won't you allow me to sit at your table? I will promise not to intrude in any way, and you may possibly be saved from such impertinences as that."

He pointed to the waiter, retiring discomfited, and Virginia, with a little murmur of delight, recognized Mr. Mildmay standing before her.

"Mr. Mildmay!" she exclaimed, holding out her hand. "Why, how glad I am to see you again!"

"And I you, Miss Longworth," he answered heartily, "but to be frank with you, I would rather have met you somewhere else."

The colour which had suddenly streamed into her cheeks faded away, and she sighed. Tall, and very immaculate in the neat simplicity of his severe evening dress, he seemed to her a more formidable person than ever he had done on the steamer. The disapproval, too, which he felt, he could scarcely help showing in some measure in his face.

"Perhaps," she said, "I ought not to have asked you to do anything so compromising as to sit with me. Please don't hesitate to say so if you would rather not."

He seated himself by her side and drew the carte toward him.

"Have you ordered?" he asked.

She nodded.

"I am so sorry," she said, "but I am in no hurry. You can catch me up." He ordered something from the waiter who was standing by, and then turned again to her.

"You mustn't be unfair to me, please," he said. "It is only because I hate to see you subjected to such affronts, that I have any feeling in the matter at all. Couldn't you have a companion, or something of that sort, if you must come to these places?"

She laughed softly.

"No!" she said, "I am afraid I couldn't do that, but if it really gives you any satisfaction to hear it, I think that my search—I told you that I had come to look for some one, didn't I?—will be over to-night, and then it will not be necessary for me to do this sort of thing."

"I am glad," he answered heartily. "I am glad, that is to say, unless—"

"Unless what?"

"Unless it means your going back to America."

She raised her eyes to his.

"And how does that concern you?" she asked, simply.

"I wish to God I knew why it should!" he answered, almost bitterly. "Do you know what a fool I have been making of myself for the last week or so? I have given up my club and all my friends, refused every invitation, and spent all my time going about from restaurant to restaurant, café to café, hoping somewhere to come across *you*."

"Mr. Mildmay!"—she began.

"Oh! you need not look like that," he interrupted. "It's perfectly true. I think you knew it upon the steamer. I suppose that last day I made myself a nuisance to you, with my advice and fears, and all that sort of thing. Well, you see, now I ask no questions. I am content to take you as you are. You want some one to look after you, Virginia. Will you marry me?"

She set down her glass, which was half raised to her lips, and looked at him with wide open eyes and trembling lips.

CHAPTER VII.
AN APPOINTMENT

Virginia seemed to find speech impossible, and it seemed to him that he could see the tears gathering in her eyes.

"Forgive me," he said, leaning over the table towards her. "I ought to have asked you differently, I know, but I am so afraid that you will slip away, as you did before, and that I shall lose sight of you again. You want some one to take care of you, dear, and I am going to do it."

She looked at him with swimming eyes, and he laid his hand softly for a moment upon hers.

"Mr. Mildmay," she said, "you must not say such things to me. It is quite impossible, entirely and absolutely impossible."

"I don't believe it," he answered calmly. "You will have to give me some very good reasons before I go away again and leave you."

"Reasons!" she faltered. "Oh! there is every reason in the world. You don't know me, or anything about me, and you know very well that I am doing things here that no nice girl would do."

"I know nothing of the sort," he answered, smiling, "because you are a nice girl. But, on the other hand, of course, I am glad to hear that your search, whatever it may be, is over. You can tell me about it or not, just as you please. Perhaps I may be able to help. Perhaps you would like to tell me. If not, it doesn't matter."

She found speech difficult, almost impossible. He seemed so sure of his position, so absolutely confident that there could be nothing which could possibly separate them.

"But you don't understand," she tried to say. "I am not the sort of person at all whom you ought to think of marrying. I am very, very poor, and I am over here because I betrayed a trust, to try and steal back something which was lost through my carelessness. I might be put in prison for what I am trying to do. All sorts of things might happen to me. You mustn't have anything to do with me."

He smiled, and rested his hand for a moment once more upon her thin white fingers.

"Little girl," he said, "I believe in you, and that is quite enough. I shall get a special license to-morrow."

She laughed a little hysterically.

"Forgive me," she said, wiping her eyes, "but over in New York they call Englishmen slow. How dare you talk of special licenses, when I have told you that I cannot, that I will not even think of marrying you!"

He looked at her with sudden keenness.

"Is there any one else?" he asked gravely.

She was forced to speak the truth.

"No, there is no one!" she said.

"Good!" he answered. "I thought not. As a matter of form, have you any further reasons why you won't marry me?"

"I don't—care for you enough," she gasped.

"You will very soon," he answered reassuringly. "I really can make myself quite an agreeable companion. You haven't seen enough of me yet. Of course I know I'm rather taking you by storm, but I am not going to leave you alone in a strange city, indulging in some melodramatic game of hide and seek. You don't need to do that, Virginia. I am quite as rich as ever you will want to be, and if any one has suffered in America through your carelessness I think I can make amends for you more completely than you can by trying to break the laws of this country. You know, dear, I am not curious, but I really think you had better tell me all about it. It will make things much easier."

She shook her head.

"It isn't my secret," she answered, "and besides, it's a dangerous one. Whoever has the paper which was stolen through my carelessness, and which I am going to try and get back, goes every moment in danger of his life."

He smiled at her a little unbelievingly.

"That may be all very well in New York," he said, "but here in London one doesn't do such things. One keeps the law here, for we have an incorruptible police."

"You don't understand," she said sadly. "This is really something great."

"Can't you buy this paper or whatever it is?" he asked, "or rather couldn't I buy it for you?"

She shook her head.

"The man who has it refused a million dollars for it," she said simply. "Indeed, I must not tell you anything more. Please, Mr. Mildmay—"

"Guy!" he interrupted.

"Guy, then," she continued, with something very much like a blush, "forget all that you have said to me, at any rate for the present. Perhaps later on, when this is all over—"

"You won't want me then," he said. "It's just now you need some one to look after you. You are too young, and forgive me, dear, too simple, to be mixed up in such affairs as you have been speaking of. There is only one way to really protect you, and that is to get that special license to-morrow."

"But you mustn't talk about it, think about it even," she protested. "It's impossible."

"No, I think not!" he answered. "Come, I am going to make you drink a glass of my wine. You are looking positively woebegone. That's right, drink it down," he added, as she sipped it timidly. "Now tell me what you are going to do for the rest of the evening."

"I am going," she said, "to try and save the life of the man who has the paper which was stolen from me. Incidentally I may be able to get it back again."

"Can I come too?" he asked.

"Certainly not!" she answered. "It isn't an affair for you to be mixed up in, and besides it would spoil my chance."

"You are not encouraging," he said. "Seriously, Virginia, do let me come."

"No!" she answered, glancing at the clock, "and I must be going in a very few minutes."

"You haven't told me yet when you will marry me," he reminded her.

She looked at him piteously.

"Please don't be foolish," she said, "I cannot marry you; I can never marry you. I told you that before. You must please put it out of your head. I am going now, and it must be"—her voice trembled a little—"good-bye!"

"It will be nothing of the sort," he answered. "Do you care for me a little, Virginia?"

"I—perhaps I do," she faltered.

"I thought you did," he whispered, smiling. "I hoped so, anyhow. That settles it, Virginia. You haven't a chance of getting away from me, dear. You may just as well make up your mind to be Mrs. Mildmay as soon as I can get that license."

"You are the most impossible person!" she declared in despair.

"How can I make you believe me?"

"Nohow," he answered. "Let me come with you, please, this evening."

"I will not," she answered firmly. "Do believe me, please, that it is impossible."

"Very well, then," he answered, "you shall have your own way, but on one condition, and that is that you tell me where I can find you to-morrow. I shall probably have the license then."

Virginia looked around the room as though seeking for some means of escape, and yet she knew that every word he uttered was a delight to her; that a new joy, against which she was powerless to fight, was filling her life. It was absurd, impossible, not to be thought of, and yet all the time his insistence delighted her. He had so much the air of one who has always his own way. She felt her powers of resistance becoming almost impotent, and she watched their dissipation with secret joy. How was it possible to resist a lover so confident, so authoritative, especially when her whole heart was filled with a passionate longing to throw everything else to the winds and to place her hands in his. Perhaps by to-morrow, she thought, things would seem different to her, but in the meantime she gave him the address of the boarding-house in Russell Street. How could she help it!

"I shall be there," he said, " sometime before twelve to-morrow morning.

You won't be going out before then?"

"I—suppose not," she faltered.

He called the waiter and asked for the bill for his dinner. Hers she had already paid. She rose to her feet.

"Please," she said earnestly, "do not come out with me. I am going now, and where I am going I must go alone."

He glanced opposite, to where the three men were still sitting.

"Very well," he said, "I will let you go. You will permit me, I presume, to see you out of the restaurant?"

He walked down with her to the door, and would have called a hansom, but she answered that she preferred to walk.

"I have an automobile here if you will use it," he said, "and I will engage not to ask the man where he drove you."

"I am not afraid of that," she answered, "but I would rather walk, if you please. I have only a very little way to go."

He took both her hands in his firmly.

"Virginia, dear," he said, smiling down at her, "good night, and remember that I am coming to see you to-morrow, and that I am going to bring that special license. You are going to marry me whether you want to or not, and very soon too."

Virginia hurried away, breathless.

CHAPTER VIII.
DEFEATED

Virginia drew a little breath of relief. After all it had been very easy. She had simply walked into the flats, entered the lift, ascended to the fifth floor, opened the door of No. 57, and walked in. She had had a moment of fear lest there should be a servant in the rooms, but it was a fear which proved groundless. She had found herself in a tiny hall, with closed doors in front and on the right of her, and an open one on the left leading into a small, plainly furnished but comfortable sitting-room. This she entered, and closed the door behind her. At last she was in Norris Vine's sanctum.

She drew a little breath, half of relief, half of excitement, and then repenting at the closed door, quietly opened it, and left it about a foot ajar. She looked round the room with a swift comprehensive glance. There was only one place where it seemed possible that papers of importance might be hidden, a small desk with pigeon-holes, before the window. She sat down in front of it, and methodically, one by one, she examined every paper she found, bills, receipts, prospectuses, charitable appeals, circulars, memoranda of literary matter. She found many of these, but nothing in the least like the paper for which she was in search.

With a little sigh she closed the desk, and, turning away from it, seated herself in the easy-chair in front of the fireplace. Almost as she did so she received a shock which sent the blood tingling through her body. The outer door had opened very softly. She had the idea that some one was standing outside hesitating whether to enter. Thoughts flashed quickly through her mind. This was not Norris Vine, or he would have entered his own room without hesitation. She affected to be absorbed in the magazine which she had picked up, but it was almost certain, from the fact that the door was gently pushed open another inch or two, that some one was looking through the chink. She read on unmoved, although she even fancied that she could hear the stifled breathing of some one peering into the room. Then she heard the door of the room outside, his bedroom without a doubt, softly opened. The intruder, whoever he might be, had evidently stolen in there.

Virginia laid down her magazine for a moment, and with half-closed eyes tried to think. Within the next room, only a few yards away, and nearer to the door leading into the flat than she herself was, was hiding the person who for two thousand five hundred pounds was proposing to rid the world of Norris Vine. What would happen if she sat still? If Norris Vine should come in, and it was almost the time at which he was expected, his assailant would probably be waiting behind the door. She had no doubt but that the attack would be swift and sudden, and that once made some means would be taken to keep her a prisoner in the room where she now was, or perhaps there might be even worse things in store for her. In any case, within a few yards of her a man lay in hiding with murder in his heart, and between them the closed door which might at any moment be opened. What chance would she have to warn Norris Vine? None at all!

She rose to her feet and sat down again. The very thought of moving nearer to the room where this man was waiting filled her with horror, and yet it was surely as dangerous to remain where she was, too far away to warn any one entering, and herself at the mercy of the conqueror in the brief struggle. Her breath began to come more quickly as she realized that she was trapped. Probably that man in the next room knew all about her, knew just why she was there, and had made up his mind how to deal with her. She found herself listening in ever-deepening horror for that turn of the handle which should signal the coming of the man for whom they both waited. Intervention of any sort would be welcome. An intervention came, in a manner as commonplace as it was startling. The bell of a telephone instrument on the top of the desk began to ring. A moment's breathless indecision, and then she walked to the instrument and took the receiver in her hand. Simultaneously she heard a stealthy movement outside. Her fellow-watcher, whoever he might be, had also made up his mind to know who was ringing up Norris Vine so late.

"Who's that?" the voice asked abruptly.

"Coniston Mansions, No. 57," Virginia answered, disguising her voice as much as possible.

"Yes! but who is it in my rooms? That isn't Janion's voice, is it?"

Then Virginia knew that the person who spoke was Norris Vine himself, and before every word she uttered she hesitated, thinking always of the listener outside.

"No, it's not Janion," she answered. "What do you want?"

"I wanted to know whether my servant was there," the voice replied. "Who are you, and what are you doing in my rooms?"

"Gone into the country?" Virginia said, speaking in a loud tone of surprise. "You mean that he will not be here to-night, after all?"

The voice down the telephone came angry and perplexed.

"What the devil are you talking about?" it asked. "I am Norris Vine, and I am speaking into my own rooms. I want to know who you are, and what you are doing there."

"Then I think," Virginia continued, still speaking loudly, "that you might be a little more careful before you send me on a fool's errand like this. Here have I been waiting for half an hour for a man who you declared was certain to come here before eleven o'clock. Now you tell me that he is not returning to-night at all, gone into the country, or some rubbish. Why can't you make sure of your facts? You seem to repeat any stuff that's told you, and then think that it doesn't matter so long as you say that you're sorry. How about my wasted time sitting here, to say nothing of the risk of being taken for a thief!"

"If you don't tell me who you are at once," the voice came back, "I shall send a policeman round. Can't you understand that I want my man Janion? I want him to bring my evening clothes to the club. If you don't tell me who you are, and what you are doing in my rooms, I shall be round there with a policeman in five minutes."

"Of course I shan't stop," Virginia replied, still in a loud voice. "What on earth is there to stop for if the man isn't coming back for several days? I shall be away before the police can come. Ring off, please."

"I don't know who the devil you are," the voice came back, "but I jolly soon will. You'll have to hurry, my friend, if you mean to get away. I am going to ring up the manager's office."

Virginia threw down the receiver. She hesitated for a moment before the looking-glass, as though straightening her hat—in reality to give the listener outside time to get back once more into hiding. Then she walked with fast beating heart and steady footsteps towards the door. She opened it boldly. The little hall was empty; the door of the room opposite, which had been closed when she had entered, was ajar now, but there were no signs of any living person. She opened the door leading into the corridor and safety. For the first time she noticed that the key was in the inside. She withdrew it, passed out, closed the door, and stood in safety in the corridor. Thoughts chased one another through her mind. She had only to lock the door on the outside, call for help, and the person who had waited with her for Norris Vine's return was caught in a trap. Would there be any advantage in it? Would she be able to clear herself?

Reluctantly she decided that it was better to let him go. She rang for the lift, and then turned with fascinated eyes to watch the door leading into Norris Vine's apartments. The lights were very dim on the landing. There were no servants or any one about. She watched the closed door with fascinated eyes. What if it should open before the lift came! She rang again, kept her finger upon the bell; then with a great sense of relief she heard the creaking of the wire rope, and saw the top of the lift beginning to ascend. It drew level with her, and the page-boy threw open the iron door. Almost at that moment she saw the door of Norris Vine's apartment softly opened from the inside. She sank down upon the seat.

"Down, please!" she said, and the lift began to descend. Her safety was assured. She turned to the boy. "Does Mr. Vine generally come up this way to his rooms?" she asked.

"Always at night, miss," the boy answered. "The other lift don't run after eleven."

She reached the hall. The commissionaire opened the doors and she passed out into the street. She crossed the road, and stood perfectly still watching the entrance. Five, ten minutes passed; then a man came out in evening dress, with silk hat, and a white handkerchief around his neck. He was smoking a cigarette, and he carried a silver-headed cane. Virginia crossed the road once more, and, trusting to the crowd, kept within a few yards of him. He turned to the edge of the curb and called a hansom.

"Claridge's Hotel!" he said. "As quick as you can, cabby!"

She gave a little start. Not only had she recognized the voice of the man who had sat behind her in the café that afternoon, but she also knew at once that this was one of the three men who had sat opposite her only an hour or so ago at dinner!

CHAPTER IX.
INGRATITUDE

Norris Vine stood in the middle of his room, his hat still upon his head, and his overcoat on his arm. Before him stood the waiter and the watchman of the flats.

"My rooms," he was saying, "have been occupied within the last ten minutes by strangers, and by people who have no right here whatever. I have certain proof of this. Do you allow any one who chooses to come into the building and use the lift, and enter whatever apartment they choose?"

"We cannot employ detectives," the manager answered, "and every one who lives here has visitors."

There was a soft knock at the door, and almost immediately it was opened. Virginia entered, and guessed immediately the meaning of the little scene before her.

"You want an explanation as to that telephone message," she said quietly. "I have come to give it to you. If you will send these people away, I will explain everything."

Norris Vine looked at her in amazement. Her face somehow seemed familiar, but he failed at first to place her. The two men whom Vine was interviewing were only too glad of the opportunity to take their departure.

"Am I to understand," Vine asked, "that it was you whose voice I heard at the telephone?"

"You are," Virginia answered, "and you may be very thankful for it. I do not know whether it was wise of me or not, but I am quite sure that I saved your life."

"In which case," Vine remarked, with an incredulous smile, "I must at least ask you to sit down."

Virginia seated herself and pushed back her veil.

"You do not remember me," she said. "I am Phineas Duge's niece."

"I remember you now quite well," he answered. "You were having dinner with your uncle one night at Sherry's."

She nodded.

"That is quite true," she said. "I have been looking for you for some days. In fact, I came to London to look for you."

"That," he remarked drily, "sounds somewhat mysterious, considering that I have not yet had the pleasure of your acquaintance."

"There is nothing mysterious about it," she answered. "You are a receiver of stolen goods. Some papers were stolen from my uncle's study by Stella, my cousin, and given to you. They were stolen through my carelessness. Unless I can recover them I am ruined."

"Go on," Morris Vine said. "You have not finished yet."

"No!" she answered, "I have not. I followed you to England to get those papers back, either by theft, or by appealing to your sense of honour, or by any means which presented themselves. I found by accident that I was not the only American in London who was over here in search of you. This afternoon I overheard part of a plot in a café in Regent Street between two men, strangers to me, but who had both apparently made up their minds that this particular paper was worth a little more than your life. From them I heard your address. Your valet must be in their pay, for they knew exactly your movements for the night. I heard them plan to come here, and I knew what the end of that would be. I determined to anticipate them. It was not out of any feeling for you, but simply because if the paper got into their hands my cause was lost. So I came on here to warn you, but I had scarcely entered your room before I was aware that some one who had come with very different intentions was already here. We waited—I in the sitting-room, he in that bedroom—waited for you. I pretended to be unconscious of his existence. He seemed to be content to ignore mine. While I was wondering how I should warn you, the telephone bell rang. I answered it, and it was you who spoke. Then I had the idea of carrying on some imaginary conversation with you, which would induce the man who was listening to go away. I did it and he went away. It must have sounded terrible nonsense to you, of course, but it was the only way I could think of to get him out of the place. He left convinced that you were not coming here to-night."

"Do you know who he was, this man?" Vine asked.

"I do not," she answered, "but I can guess who his employers are."

"And so can I," Vine said grimly. "It seems to me that you are a very plucky young lady, Miss Longworth."

"Not at all," she answered. "What I have done, I have done for the sake of reward."

"Will you name it?" he asked.

"I want that paper to take back to my uncle," she said. "Stella stole it from me brutally, and unless I can get it back again, my uncle is going to send me back to the little farmhouse where I came from, and is going to leave off helping my people. I want that paper back, Mr. Vine, and you must give it to me."

He looked at her with utterly impassive face.

"I am afraid, Miss Longworth," he said, "that I must disappoint you. If I gave you back that paper, it would go into the hands of one of the most unprincipled men in America. It is not only your uncle whom I dislike, but his methods, his craft, his infernal, incarnate selfishness. He wants this paper as a whip to hold over other people. He obtained it by subtlety. The means by which it was taken from him, although I had nothing to do with them, were on the whole justified. I cannot give it back to you, Miss Longworth. I have not made up my mind yet what to do with it, and I certainly have no friendship for the men whom it implicates; but all the same, for the present it must remain in my possession."

"Do you know," she reminded him, "that I have saved your life to-night?"

He laughed softly.

"My dear child," he said, "my life is not so easily disposed of. I believe that you have tried to do me a kindness, but you ask too great a return. Even if the paper you speak of was stolen, it is better in my keeping than in your uncle's."

"You will not give it to me, then?" she asked.

"I will not," he answered.

She rose from her place.

"Very well," she said; "I am going now, but I think that we shall meet again before very long."

He opened the door for her and walked out toward the lift.

"My dear young lady," he said, "I hope you will forgive my saying so, but this is certainly a wild-goose chase of yours. If you will take my advice, and I know something about life, you will go back to your farmhouse in the Connecticut valley. These larger places in the world may seem fascinating to you at first, but believe me you will be better off and happier in the backwoods. Ask Stella. I think that she would give you the same advice."

Virginia looked at him steadily. The faint note of sarcasm which was seldom absent from his tone was not lost upon her.

"I thank you for your advice," she said, "It sounds so disinterested — and convincing. Such an excellent return, too, for a person who has risked something to do you a kindness."

"My dear young lady," Vine answered, "it was not for my own sake that you warned me. You have admitted that yourself. It was entirely from your own point of view that you judged it well for me to remain a little longer on the earth. Why, therefore, should I be grateful? As a matter of fact, I am not sure that I am. I, too, go about armed, and it is by no means certain that I might not have had the best of any little encounter with our friend who you say was hiding there." — He motioned his head towards his bedroom. — "In that case, you see, I should have known exactly who he was, possibly even have been able to hand him over to the police."

Virginia pressed the little bell and the lift began to ascend.

"I am glad to know, Mr. Vine," she said, "what sort of a man you are."

He bowed, and she stepped into the lift without any further form of farewell. Vine walked thoughtfully back to his rooms. He was a man who had grown hard and callous in the stress of life, but somehow the memory of Virginia's pale face and dark reproachful eyes remained with him.

CHAPTER X.
A NEW VENTURE

Phineas Duge, notwithstanding an absence of anything approaching vulgarity in his somewhat complex disposition, was, for a man of affairs and an American, singularly fond of the small elegances of life. Although he sat alone at dinner, the table was heaped with choice flowers and carefully selected hothouse fruit. His one glass of wine, the best of its sort, he sipped meditatively, and with the air of a connoisseur. The soft lights upon the table were such as a woman, mindful of her complexion, might have chosen. Behind his chair stood his English butler, grave, solemn-faced, attentive. The cigars and matches were already on his left-hand side, ready for the moment when he should have finished his wine. Outside a footman was waiting for a signal to bring in the after-dinner coffee.

Across his luxurious table, through the waving clusters of sweet-smelling flowers to the dark mahogany panelled wall beyond, the eyes of Phineas Duge seemed to be seeking that night something which they failed to find. The last few weeks seemed in a way to have aged the man. His lips had come closer together, there were faint lines on his forehead and underneath his eyes. The butler from behind his chair looked down upon his master's carefully parted and picturesque hair, wondering why he sat so still, wondering what he saw that he looked so steadily at that one particular spot in the panelled wall, and lingered so unusually long over the last few drops of his wine. Phineas Duge himself wondered still more what had come to him. For many years men and women had come and gone, leaving him indifferent as to their coming and going, their pains and their joys; and to-night, though there were many matters with which his mind might well have been occupied, he found himself in the curious position of indulging in vague and almost regretful memories. The place at the other end of his table was empty, as it had been for many nights; for during the period of his titanic struggle with those men against whom he had declared war, he had shunned all society, and lived a life of stern and absolute seclusion.

To-night that steady gaze which wandered over the drooping flowers was really fixed upon that empty chair at the other end of the table. A man of few fancies, he was never quite without imagination. His thoughts had travelled easily back to a few weeks ago. He saw Virginia sitting there, watched the delightful smile coming and going, the large grey eyes that watched him so ceaselessly, the little ripple of pleasant conversation, which he had never dreamed that he could ever miss. After all, what a child! As a matter of justice, and he told himself that it was justice only which had power to sway his judgment, what right had he to blame her for what was really nothing but a freak of ill-fortune! Had he punished himself in sending her away? Somehow, during these last few nights, the room had seemed curiously cold and empty. He had missed her little timidly offered ministrations, the touch of her fingers upon his shoulder, the whole nameless delicacy which her presence had brought into the cold, magnificent surroundings, which seemed to him now as though they could never be quite the same again.

These thoughts had come to him before, but it was only to-night he had suffered them to linger in his mind. Once or twice he had caught them lurking in his brain and thrown them out. To-night they had come with a soft, invincible persistence, so that he had felt even his will powerless to strangle them. He was forced to face the truth, that he, Phineas Duge, the man of many millions, sat there while the minutes fled past, looking with empty eyes into empty space, thinking of the child whom he would have given at that moment more than he would have cared to confess, to have found sitting within a few feet of him, peeling his walnuts, or pouring out her impressions of this wonderful new life into which she had come.

Some trifle it was which broke the thread of his reflections. When he realized what he had been doing, he was conscious of a feeling almost of shame. In a moment he was himself again. He calmly drank up his wine, and as he set the glass down held out a cigar from the box to the man who waited with the cigar cutter in hand. A little silver spirit lamp burning with a blue flame stood all ready at his elbow. The butler gave the signal, and his coffee, strong and fragrant, in a little gold cup, was placed before him.

"You will tell Smedley to be in the study at nine o'clock," he ordered.

"Very good, sir!" the man replied. "You will not be going out to-night, sir? There are no orders for the garage?"

"Not to-night," Phineas Duge answered.

There was an unexpected sound of voices outside in the hall. Phineas Duge looked toward the door with a frown upon his face.

"What is that?" he asked sharply.

The butler was perplexed.

"I will go and see, sir," he said. "It sounds as if James were having trouble with some one."

The door was suddenly opened. Weiss and Higgins entered quickly, followed by the protesting and frightened footman. Phineas Duge rose from his seat, and, resting one hand upon the table, peered forward at the two men. His face, even under the rose-shaded electric lamp, was cold and set. The gleam of white teeth was visible between his lips. He looked like a man, metaphorically, about to spring upon his foes. One hand had stolen round to the pocket of his dinner coat, and was holding something hard, but to him very comforting. He offered no word of greeting. He uttered no exclamation of surprise. He simply waited.

"These gentlemen pushed past me in the hall, sir," the footman explained, deprecatingly. "My back was turned only for a moment, and Wilkins was down having his supper."

"You can go," Phineas Duge said coldly, waving him out of the room. "What do you want with me, Weiss?"

"A few minutes' sensible talk," Weiss answered. "It will do you no harm to listen to us. Send your servant away and give us a quarter of an hour."

Phineas Duge hesitated, but only for a moment. These men had come openly, and they were known to be his enemies. It was not possible that they intended to use any violence. He turned to the butler, who stood behind his chair.

"Place chairs for these gentlemen," he ordered, "and leave the room."

They sat on his left-hand side, Phineas Duge pushed the decanter of Burgundy toward them, and the cigars. Then he leaned back in his chair and waited.

"Duge, we ought to have come to you before," Weiss began. "We are playing a child's game, all of us."

"Whatever the game may be," Duge answered, "it is not I who invented it."

"We grant that to start with," Weiss answered. "We were in the wrong. You have done a little better than hold your own against us. We are several millions of dollars the poorer and you the richer for our split. Let it go at that. We have other things to think about just now besides this juggling with markets. I take it that we are none of us particularly anxious to learn what the interior of a police court looks like."

Phineas Duge made no motion of assent or dissent.

"You refer," he said, "to the action against the Trusts which the President is supposed to be supporting so vigorously?"

Weiss nodded.

"The thing's further advanced than we were any of us inclined to believe," he answered. "Every one of us is interested in this, you more than any of us. If Harrison's Bill passes the Senate, we are liable to imprisonment at any moment. We are up against it hard, Duge, and we can't face it as we ought while we're squabbling amongst ourselves like a set of children."

"You propose then," Phineas Duge said slowly, "to close our accounts on a mutual basis?"

"Precisely!" Weiss answered. "You have had the best of it, and it might be our turn to-morrow, so you can well afford to do this. We want to rest on our oars for a time, while we look round and face this new danger."

"Very well," Phineas Duge said, "I agree. We will meet at your office to-morrow and bring our brokers. I am quite willing to end this fight. It was not I who began it."

Higgins drew a little breath of relief. He was perhaps the poorest of the group, and it was his stock which Duge had been handling so roughly. "Thank heavens!" he said. "Now we can have a moment's breathing time, to see what we can do for these fellows who want to teach us how to manage our affairs."

"In the first place," Weiss said, "what about that paper we signed? I can understand your wanting to hold it over us while we were at war. It was a fair weapon, and you had a right to it, but now we are united again you can see, of course, that although your name isn't on it, it would practically mean ruin to our interests if the other side once got hold of it."

"If I had that paper," Duge said quietly, "I would tear it up at this moment, but I regret to say that I have not. It was stolen during my illness."

"We know that," Weiss answered. "We know even in whose hands it is."

Phineas Duge looked up inquiringly.

"Norris Vine has it," Weiss continued. "We have offered him a million, but he declines to sell. He would have used it for his paper before now, and we should have been on the other side of the ocean, but for the fact that John Drayton advised him not to. Now he has taken it with him to London. He is going to ask Deane's advice. At any moment the thing may come flashing back. We may wake up to find a copy of that document in black and white in every paper in New York State."

"You have offered him a reasonable sum for it," Phineas Duge said, "and he declines to sell. Very well, what do you propose to do?"

"It was stolen from you," Weiss said. "He may justly decline to treat with us; but it is your property, and you have a right to it."

"You propose, then?" Phineas Duge asked.

"That you should catch the *Kaiserin* to London to-morrow," Higgins said, "and find out this man Vine. The rest we are content to leave with you, but I think that if you try you will get it."

Phineas Duge sat quite still for several moments. He sipped his wine thoughtfully, threw his cigar, which had gone out, into the fire, and lit a cigarette. He appreciated the force of the suggestion, and a trip to Europe was by no means distasteful to him, but he was not a man to decide upon anything of this sort without reflection.

"A week ago," he said softly, "even a day ago, and my absence from New York would have meant ruin. If I leave the country to-morrow, and trust myself upon the ocean for six days, what guarantee have I that you will keep to any arrangement which we might make to-morrow?"

"We will sign affidavits," Weiss declared, "that we will not, directly or indirectly, enter into any operations in any one of our stocks during your absence, except for your profit as well as our own. We will execute a deed of partnership as regards any transactions which we might enter into during your absence."

Phineas Duge nodded thoughtfully.

"I suppose," he said, "we might be able to fix things up that way. I should be glad enough to get the paper back again, but Vine is not an easy man to deal with, and he is pleased to call himself my enemy."

"The men who have called themselves that," Higgins remarked grimly, "have generally been sorry for it."

"And so may he," Phineas Duge answered, "but I am not sure that his time has come yet. You must let me think this over, gentlemen, until to-morrow morning. I will meet you with my broker and lawyer at ten o'clock at your office, Weiss, and if I make up my mind to go to Europe, my luggage will be on the steamer by that time. On the whole I might tell you that I am inclined to go."

Weiss drew a great breath of relief. He poured himself out a glass of wine and drank it off.

"It's good to hear you say that, Duge," he said. "I tell you we have come pretty near being scared the last week or so. I feel a lot more comfortable fighting with you in the ranks."

Phineas Duge forbore from all recrimination. He filled Higgins' glass and his own. He could afford to be magnanimous. He had fought them one against four, and they had come to him for mercy!

"We will drink," he said, "to the new President. This one has tilted against the windmills once too often. He must learn his lesson."

CHAPTER XI.
CONSCIENCE

Virginia slept little that night. Her room, one of the smallest and least expensive in the cosmopolitan boarding-house where she was staying, was high up, almost in an attic. The windows were small, and opened with difficulty. The heat, combined with her own restlessness, made the weary hours one long nightmare for her. Early in the morning she rose and sat in front of the little window, looking out across the wilderness of house-tops, where a pall of smoke seemed to convert to luminous chaos the rising sun. There was a lump in her throat, and gathering tears in her eyes. It seemed to her that no one could ever realize a loneliness more absolute and complete than hers. She thought of the early summer mornings in that tiny farmhouse perched on the side of the lonely valley, where the air at least was clear and pure and bright, musical with the song of birds, and the west wind which stirred always in the pine-woods behind heralded the coming morning. If only she could have dropped from her shoulders the burden of the last few months, and found herself back there once more. Then a pang of remorse shook her heart. She remembered the happiness which through her had come to those whom she loved, and the thought was like a tonic to her. She forgot her own sorrows, she forgot that dim tremendous feeling, which had shown through her life for a minute or two, only to pass away and leave behind longings and regrets which were in themselves a constant pain. She forgot everything except the thought of what it might mean to those others who were dear to her if she should fail in her task. Her face seemed suddenly aged as she sat there, crushing down the sweeter things, clenching her fingers upon the window-sill, and telling herself that at any cost she must succeed, hopeless though the task might seem.

Presently she began to move about the room and collect her clothes. At half-past nine she had left the boarding-house and departed without leaving any address behind her. At ten o'clock a great automobile swung round the corner, stopped before the door, and Mr. Mildmay descended and ran lightly up the steps. Miss Longworth had gone away, he was told by the shabby German waiter in soiled linen coat and greasy black trousers. She had left no address. She had left no message for any one who might be calling for her. The largest tip which he had ever received could only send him into the inner regions to interview the proprietress, who came out and confirmed his words. Mildmay turned slowly around and drove away.

* * * * *

Stella and Norris Vine lunched together that day in a small West End restaurant. He had telephoned asking her to come, and she had at once thrown over another engagement. They were scarcely seated before he asked her a question.

"Do you know that your cousin is in London?"

"What! Virginia?" Stella exclaimed.

He nodded, and Stella was genuinely amazed.

"Whom did she come with?" she asked. "What does she want here?"

"She came alone, poor little thing," he answered, "and on a wild-goose chase. I never heard anything so pathetic in my life. She ought to be in short frocks, playing with her dolls, and she has come here four thousand miles to a city she knows nothing of, to steal back— well, you know what. One could laugh if it were not so pathetic."

"Little fool!" Stella said, half contemptuously, and yet with a note of regret in her tone.

"I thought, perhaps," Vine said, "you might find out where she is and go and talk common sense to her. If there is anything else we can do, I'd like to, only I hate the thought of a pretty child like that wandering about London on such an absurd quest."

"Do you know where she is to be found?" Stella asked quietly.

"I have no idea," Vine answered. "The last time I saw her was in my own rooms. I am only sorry that I let her go."

Stella looked up at him quickly.

"Your own rooms!" she repeated. "What do you mean?"

"Well," he answered, "with the extraordinary luck which comes sometimes to babies, she overheard two men talking about me and arranging to meet at a certain hour at my flat. She actually had the nerve to be there herself at the same time. While she sat in my sitting-room, they waited in the bedroom. Mind, a great part of this may be her invention. I have only her word for it, but she certainly seemed as though she were telling the truth. I rang up for some one to bring me a change of clothes, and she answered the telephone. What she said to me sounded such rank nonsense that I jumped in a hansom and went straight back to my rooms. However, the men who were listening gathered from what she said that I was not coming back, and they gave it up and stole out. When I returned I found her waiting there, and she demanded that I should give her up the paper she wanted as a matter of gratitude."

"Do you believe her story?" Stella asked.

"I don't know," he answered. "I know that I am being followed about, and if she could get into my rooms, it is quite as easy for them to do so. They may have been there, and I dare say that if I had entered unsuspectingly, and Dan Prince had anything to do with it, I shouldn't have had much chance. It amused me to see all my drawers turned out and my papers disturbed."

"Little idiot!" Stella said impatiently. "She ought to be at home, feeding her father's chickens. She is hopelessly out of place here, just as she was in New York,"

"I wish we could send her back there," Vine declared.

Stella looked at him with raised eyebrows.

"My dear Norris," she said, "isn't this rather a new departure for you? I don't seem to recognize you in this frame of mind."

He sipped his wine thoughtfully for a minute or two, and helped himself to some curry.

"I believe after all, Stella," he said, "that you know very little about me. I am naturally a most tender-hearted person."

"You have managed," she remarked drily, "to conceal your weakness most effectively."

"A journalist," he reminded her, "is used to conceal them. Without the arts of lying and acting, we might as well abandon our profession.

Seriously, Stella, I am sorry for the child. I wish you could find her and pack her off home."

Stella shrugged her shoulders.

"In the first place," she said, "I have no idea where to look; and in the second, she is one of those obstinate children who never do what they are told, or see reason."

"I admit," he replied, "that finding her is rather a difficulty, but after all, you see, it is you directly, and I indirectly, who are responsible for her troubles. I think we ought to do what we can. I wish I hadn't let her go the other night."

"I am becoming," Stella said, smiling, "a little jealous of my cousin."

He looked at her with steady scrutiny, as though he were curious to decide how much of truth there might be in her words.

"You have no need, my dear Stella," he said, "to be jealous of Virginia or any other girl. This is simply the dying kick of a nearly finished conscience."

"If I come across her," Stella said, "I will do what I can. If you see her again, and I should think you are the more likely, find out her address and I will go and see her. By the by," she added, leaning across the table towards him, "you seem very confident of preserving it. Tell me, where do you keep that paper?"

He smiled.

"Ah!" he said. "All my secrets save one are yours, but I think that that one I will not tell you."

She frowned at him, obviously annoyed.

"Do you mean that?" she asked. "Surely you do not hesitate to trust me?"

"Not for one moment," he answered. "On the other hand, the knowledge of a thing of that sort is better in as few hands as possible. You will be none the better for knowing. Circumstances might arise to make even the knowledge an embarrassment to you. Take my advice, and do not ask me that question."

Stella's face had grown darker.

"It is I," she said, "whom you have to thank for the possession of it. Considering that you go in danger every moment, I think that some one else save yourself should share in the knowledge of what you have done with it."

"Let me recommend," he said, studying the menu for a moment with his horn-rimmed eyeglass, "an artichoke with sauce mayonnaise, or would you prefer asparagus?"

"I should prefer," she insisted, "an answer to my question."

He looked at her steadily. His face was utterly impassive, his forefinger was tapping lightly upon the table-cloth. It was a look which she knew very well.

"The knowledge of where that paper is, Stella, would do you no good," he declared. "Forgive me, but I do not intend to tell a soul."

They finished their luncheon almost in silence. She only once recurred to the subject.

"Perhaps," she said, looking quietly up at him, "as your conscience is growing so susceptible, you will think it right to restore that paper to my little cousin. Those are wonderful eyes, of hers, you know, now she has learnt to use them a little."

Norris Vine did not answer, and they parted with the briefest of farewells.

CHAPTER XII.
DUKE OF MOWBRAY

This time Mildmay was angry. He showed it alike in his speech and expression. Virginia looked at him like a terrified child.

"So, Virginia," he said, "I have found you at last!"

"What do you want?" she asked breathlessly.

He looked at her for quite thirty seconds without replying. Her eyes fell before his. More than ever she felt the shame of her position.

"What do I want?" he repeated, a little bitterly. "You ask me that, Virginia, seriously?"

She covered her face with her hands.

"Oh! please go away," she said. "It is not kind of you to come here."

"I do not mean to be unkind," he answered, "but I want to understand. Why did you leave your boarding-house in Russell Street and run away from me?"

"It was not only to run away from you," she answered. "There were other reasons."

"Why should you wish to run away from me at all?" he asked.

"Because," she answered, "I am afraid, and you ask me things which are impossible."

"What are you afraid of?" he asked.

"Of myself, of you, of everything," she murmured pathetically.

Virginia was a little worn out. Day after day of disappointment had tried her sorely. He felt himself softening, but he showed no signs of it in his face.

"Is there anywhere here where we can talk?" he asked. "You have rooms in the building, have you not? Are you alone?"

He could have bitten his tongue out for that question, but its significance never occurred to her.

"Yes!" she answered. "Since you are here, perhaps you had better come in."

They had met on the landing of the fifth floor of Coniston Mansions. She led him down the corridor, and, opening a door, ushered him into a tiny sitting-room.

"How did you find me out?" she asked.

"I saw you dining at Luigi's yesterday and to-day," he answered sternly. "You were with the same man both times. I followed you yesterday. You both came back here. To-day you came back alone. Is this man your brother?"

"No!" she answered.

"Your cousin? Is he any relation to you?"

"No!" she repeated.

"Who is he, then?"

"A friend," she answered, "or an enemy perhaps. What does it matter to you?"

He looked at her steadfastly. She was dressed in white muslin, and she wore a big black hat without any touch of colour. Her clothes were those which her uncle had ordered in New York. She was slim and dainty and elegant, and he found it hard indeed to keep his heart steeled against her.

"How can you ask me that, Virginia?" he replied. "Have you forgotten that I have asked you to marry me?"

"And I have told you that I cannot," she replied desperately. "I cannot and I will not. You have no right to come here and worry me."

"So my coming does worry you?" he asked.

"Yes!" she answered desperately, "you know that it does."

"Virginia," he said, "what is this man's name?"

"It is no concern of yours," she answered.

"Are you in love with him?"

"I shall not tell you," she said.

"Is he in love with you?"

"If you ask me any more such questions, I shall go into my room and lock the door," she declared.

Mildmay took a turn up and down the little apartment. The child was obdurate, yet all the time he seemed to read her soft frightened eyes.

"Virginia," he said suddenly, stopping in front of her, "I have the license in my pocket. Won't you come out with me and be married?"

"No!" she answered, "I will not."

"Think!" he begged her. "It would be so easy. We could walk out of this place together, and in an hour's time you would have some one else to take your little troubles on their shoulders. Don't you think that mine are broad enough, little girt?"

"Please don't!" she begged. "I cannot. I wish you would not ask me."

"I don't know whether it makes any difference," he said, after a moment's hesitation, "but I have plenty of money. In fact I am very rich. If there is any possible way in which money could help your troubles, they would soon be over."

"Oh! I know that you have," she answered. "It is not that."

He looked at her fixedly.

"You know that I have? Perhaps you know who I am?"

"I do," she answered. "You are Guy Mildmay, Duke of Mowbray."

He was taken aback.

"How did you find that out?" he asked.

"On the steamer," she answered,
"the last few days. People got to know,
I am not sure how, and in any case it does not matter."

A light began to break in upon him.

"I believe," he said, "that it is because you know you will not marry me."

"Oh! it isn't only that," she answered. "It is utterly, absolutely impossible. My people live on a little farm in America, and have barely enough money to live on. We are terribly poor."

He frowned for a moment thoughtfully. He was looking at her expensive clothes. He did not understand.

"And besides," she continued, "there is another reason why I should never think of it. Now, please, won't you believe me and go away? It is not kind of you to make it so difficult for me."

"Very well, Virginia," he said quietly, "for the present I will ask you no more. But can you tell me any reason why I should not be your friend?"

"None at all," she answered. "You can be what you like, if you will only go away and leave me alone."

"That," he answered, "is not my idea of friendship. If we are friends, I have the right to help you in your troubles, whatever they may be."

"That," she declared, "is impossible."

Then he began to realize that this child, with her soft great eyes, her delightful mouth, her girlish face, which ever since he had first seen it had seemed to him the prototype of all that was gentle and lovable, possessed a strength of character incredible in one of her years and appearance. He realized that he was only distressing her by his presence. The timidity of her manner was no sign of weakness, and there was finality even in that earnest look which she had fixed upon him.

"You decline me as a husband then, Virginia," he said, "and you decline me as a friend. You want to have nothing more to do with me. Very well, I will go away."

She drew a sharp breath between her teeth, and if he noticed it he made no sign. He drew a paper from his pocket and calmly tore it into pieces.

"That," he said, "was the paper which was to have made us happy. Good-bye!"

"Good-bye!" she gasped, tearfully.

He laughed as he took her into his arms. She did not make the least resistance.

"You little idiot!" he said. "Do you know that I very nearly went?"

Her head was buried upon his shoulder, and she was not in the position for a moment to make any reply.

CHAPTER XIII.
AN INTRODUCTION

He helped Virginia to descend from the automobile, and led her up the steps in front of the great house in Grosvenor Square.

"You are not frightened, dear?" he asked.

"I am terrified to death," she answered frankly. He touched her hand reassuringly.

"Silly child!" he said. "I am sure you will like my aunt."

The door flew open before them. A footman stood aside to let them pass. An elderly servant in plain black clothes came hurrying down from a little office.

"I trust that your Grace is well?" he said.

"Very well indeed, thank you, Jameson," Mildmay said. "Is my aunt in?"

"Her ladyship is in the morning-room, your Grace," the man answered, with an almost imperceptible glance towards Virginia. "Shall I announce you?"

"Is she alone?" Mildmay asked.

"For the moment, yes, your Grace," the man answered.

Guy led Virginia across the hall, knocked at a door and entered. A tall, grey-haired lady was sitting on a sofa with a tea-tray by her side. She was very good-looking, and absurdly like Mildmay, to whom she held out her right hand. Guy stooped and raised it to his lips.

"My dear aunt," he said, "can you stand a shock?"

"That depends," she answered, glancing at Virginia. "My nerves are not what they were, you know. However, go on."

"I am trying you rather high, I know," he said, "but there are reasons for it which I can explain later on. I have brought a young lady to see you, Miss Virginia Longworth. I want you to like her very much, because she has promised to be my wife."

Lady Medlincourt held out her hand, long and slim and delicate, and made room for Virginia by her side on the sofa.

"How are you, my dear?" she said quite calmly. "Will you have some tea? It's beastly, I know, been standing for hours, but Guy can ring for some fresh. So you are really going to marry my nephew?"

Virginia raised her eyes, and looked for a moment into the face of the woman who sat by her side.

"Yes, Lady Medlincourt," she answered; "I do hope you will not be angry."

"Angry! My dear child, I am never angry," Lady Medlincourt declared. "I have arrived at that time in life when one cannot afford the luxury of giving way to emotion. You won't mind my asking you a few questions, though, both of you. To begin with, I do not know your name. Who are you?"

Guy leaned a little forward.

"She will be Duchess of Mowbray in a very short time, aunt," he said. "Please don't forget that."

Lady Medlincourt raised her eyebrows.

"Bless the boy!" she exclaimed. "As though I were likely to! I can feel it go shivering down my backbone all the time. Sit here for a moment, both of you. I am going to give Jameson orders myself not to admit any one for a little while."

She crossed the room and they were alone for a moment. They exchanged quick glances, and Guy laughed at the consternation in Virginia's face.

"Don't be scared, little woman," he said. "You'll get on all right with my aunt, I am sure. She is a little odd just at first, and she hates to show any feeling about anything, but she's a thundering good sort."

"She seems just a little casual, doesn't she?" Virginia asked— "rather as though you had brought me to call?"

"Don't you worry, dear," he answered, smiling. "That's only her manner.

Just drink your tea and you'll feel better."

Virginia shook her head.

"I can't, Guy," she declared. "It's just too poisonous."

"I'll ring for some fresh," he said, moving toward the bell.

"Please don't," she begged. "I hate tea anyway. Guy, you are not sorry, are you?"

He took her hand and laughed reassuringly.

"You little idiot!" he said. "Do you want me to kiss you?"

"I don't much care," Virginia answered. "I have a sort of feeling in my throat that I want—some one to kiss me. You're quite, quite sure that whatever your aunt may say you will never regret this?"

"Absolutely, positively certain!" he declared. "And you?"

"It isn't the same thing with me," Virginia declared, shaking her head. "I am not going to marry a pig in a poke."

"It's a very dear little pig," he said, resting his hand for a moment upon her shoulder.

Lady Medlincourt reappeared. She resumed her seat, and motioned Guy to sit opposite to her.

"Now we shall not be disturbed for at least a quarter of an hour," she said, "and I want to hear all about it. You are very pretty, I am glad to see, dear," she said, looking at Virginia contemplatively. "I hate plain girls. What did you say that your name was?"

"Virginia Longworth!" Virginia answered, blushing.

"Quite a charming name!" Lady Medlincourt said, shutting her eyeglasses with a snap. "Tell me all about her, Guy."

"My dear aunt," he answered, laughing, "we aren't married yet."

Lady Medlincourt nodded.

"Ah!" she said. "No doubt you'll have plenty to discover later on. Put it another way. Tell me the things that I must know about the Duchess of Mowbray."

"As for instance?" he asked quietly.

"Her people," Lady Medlincourt said. "You are American, I suppose, child?" she continued. "You have very little accent, but I fancy that I can just detect it, and we don't see eyes like yours in England."

"Yes, I am American, Lady Medlincourt," Virginia answered.

"Who are your people, then?" Lady Medlincourt asked. "Where did you meet? Who introduced you? Don't look at one another like a pair of stupids. Remember that, however pointed my questions may sound, they are things which I must know if I am to be of any use to you."

Virginia went a little pale.

"Lady Medlincourt," she said, "I am sorry, but I cannot answer any questions just now."

Lady Medlincourt drew back a little in her place. She looked at the girl in frank amazement.

"What!" she exclaimed.

Guy leaned forward in his chair.

"Dear aunt," he pleaded, "don't think that we are both mad, but I have promised Virginia that she shan't be bothered with questions for a short time. I met her on the steamer coming over from America, and that is all we can tell you just now."

Lady Medlincourt looked from one to the other. She was more than a trifle bewildered.

"Bless the boy!" she exclaimed. "You don't call this bothering her with questions, do you? She can tell me about her people, can't she?"

"Her people," he answered firmly, "are going to be my people."

Lady Medlincourt gasped.

"You have known her, then," she said, "about three weeks?"

"I have known her long enough to realize that she is the girl whom I have been waiting for all my life."

Lady Medlincourt shrugged her shoulders.

"All your life!" she exclaimed impatiently. "Twenty-eight silly years! Have you nothing more to say to me than this, either of you? Do you seriously mean that you bring this very charming young lady here, and ask me to accept her as your fiancée, without a single word of explanation as to her antecedents, who she is, or where she came from?"

Virginia rose to her feet.

"Guy," she said, turning towards him, "we ought never to have come here. Lady Medlincourt has a perfect right to ask these questions. Until we can answer them we ought to go away."

Guy took her hand in his.

"Aunt," he said, "can't you trust a little in my judgment? Look at her. She is the girl whom I love, and whom I am going to trust with my name. Can't you let it go at that for the present?"

Lady Medlincourt shook her head.

"No, I cannot, Guy!" she said, "and if you weren't a silly fool you would not ask me. The future Duchess of Mowbray has to explain her position, whether she is a gentlewoman or a chorus girl. There's plenty of rope for her nowadays. She may be pretty well anything she pleases, but she must be some one. Don't think I am a brute, dear," she added, turning not unkindly to Virginia. "I like your appearance all right, and I dare say we could be friends. But if you wish me to accept you as my nephew's future wife, you must remember that the position which he is giving you is one that has its obligations as well as its pleasures. You'll have to open your pretty little mouth, or I am afraid I can't do anything for you."

Virginia turned to Guy.

"Your aunt is quite right," she said. "I know it must sound very foolish, but I came over here on an errand which I cannot tell any one about just yet."

"That, of course, is for you to decide," Lady Medlincourt said, rising, "but I wouldn't be silly about it if I were you. I must go and change my gown, as I have some people coming for bridge. Supposing you show her the house, Guy, and when I come back perhaps both of you may have changed your minds and be a little more reasonable. Remember," she added, turning to Virginia, "that I am quite serious in what I say. It will give me very great pleasure to be of any possible use to the affianced wife of my favourite nephew, but there must be no secrets. I hate secrets, especially about women. If your father is a market-gardener it's all right, so long as you can explain exactly who you are and where you came from; but there must be no mystery. Talk it over with her, Guy. I'll look in here on my way out."

She nodded a little curtly but not unkindly, and swept toward the door, which Guy opened and closed after her. Then he came slowly back, and, putting his arm around Virginia's waist, kissed her.

"You don't want to see the house, do you?" he asked.

Virginia shook her head.

"Not a bit," she answered. "I think that we had better go away."

"There is no hurry," he answered slowly. "We may as well stay and talk it over a bit. When one comes to think of it, it is trying the old lady pretty high, isn't it? Suppose we just review the situation for a minute or two. Something might occur to us."

Virginia leaned back against the cushions.

"Certainly," she answered. "You review it and I'll listen."

"Right!" Guy answered. "I met you first, then, never mind exactly how long ago, on the steamer coming from America. You were quite alone, unescorted, and unchaperoned. That in itself, as of course you know, was a very remarkable thing. Nevertheless, I think you will admit that it did not terrify me. We became—well, pretty good friends, didn't we?"

"I think we did," she admitted.

"Afterwards," he continued, "we met again at Luigi's restaurant. There again I found you alone, in a restaurant where the women who know what they are doing would not dream of entering without a proper escort. Forgive me, but I want you to understand the position thoroughly. I saw, of course, that you were being annoyed by the attentions of almost every man who entered the place, and in my very best manner I came over and made a suggestion."

Virginia sighed.

"You did it very nicely," she murmured.

"I rather flatter myself," he continued, "that I showed tact. I asked simply to be allowed to sit at your table. Before we had finished dinner I asked you, for the second time, to marry me."

"That," she declared, "was distinctly forward."

"You will remember that I refused to discuss things with you then. I told you that I was coming for you the next morning, and I mentioned what I thought of bringing with me. When I arrived at your boarding-house you had gone. You left no word nor any message. I don't consider that that was treating me nicely."

"It wasn't," she admitted, "but you have forgiven me for it."

He nodded.

"Of course I have. Well, a few nights later I saw you dining with a man whom I know slightly, a clever fellow, distinctly a man of the world. You were dining with him alone. I followed you home to Coniston Mansions. Then I came away, and hesitated for some time whether to get drunk or go for a swim in the Thames. Eventually I went home to bed."

"It was very sensible," she murmured.

"The next night," he continued, "you were dining with the same man again, only this time he did not go back with you to Coniston Mansions. I did, and before I left you, you had promised to be my wife. You warned me to ask you no questions, and I didn't. I know as little of you now as I did on the steamer. I know that this man Norris Vine has a flat within a few yards of yours, and in the same building, but I ask no questions. I think that you must certainly acquit me of anything in the shape of undue curiosity. I was content to know that I had fallen in love with the sweetest little girl I had ever set eyes on."

She pressed his hand and sighed.

"Guy, you're a dear!" she said.

"It was quite sufficient for me," he continued, "that you are what you are. It is sufficient for me even now. The trouble is that it won't be sufficient for everybody. You can see that for yourself, dear, can't you?"

Virginia drew a little away. He fancied that the hand which still rested in his was growing colder.

"I suppose so," she murmured.

"I am glad you realize that," Guy said earnestly. "Now look here, Virginia. You saw the line my aunt took. There's no doubt that from a certain point of view she's right. I wonder whether, under the circumstances, it would be better"—he hesitated, and looked at her for a moment—"better—you see what I mean, don't you?"

"I am not quite sure," she said. "Hadn't you better tell me?"

Guy looked at her in surprise.

"Why, that was just what I thought I had done," he declared. "What I mean is that after all, although for my own sake I wouldn't ask a question, it might be as well for you to tell my aunt what she wants to know. It would make things much more comfortable."

"I think you are quite right," Virginia said softly.

Guy stooped and kissed her.

"Dear little lady!" he declared. "I'll go and tell her, and bring her back."

He found his aunt descending the stairs, but when they reached the morning-room it was empty. Guy looked around in surprise, and stepped out into the hall. Jameson hurried up to him.

"The young lady has just gone, sir," he said deferentially. "I called a hansom for her myself. She seemed rather in a hurry."

Guy stood for a moment motionless.

"Do you happen to remember the address she gave you?" he asked the man.

"I am sorry, your Grace. I did not hear it."

Lady Medlincourt opened the door of the morning-room.

"I think, Guy," she said, "you had better come in and talk to me."

CHAPTER XIV.
ANOTHER DISAPPEARANCE

It was between half-past four and five o'clock in the morning, and London for the most part slept. Down in the street below, the roar of traffic, which hour after hour had grown less and less, had now died away. Within the building itself every one seemed asleep. Floor after floor looked exactly the same. The lights along the corridors were burning dimly. Every door was closed except the door of the service-room, in which a sleepy waiter lay upon a couch and dreamed of his Fatherland. The lift had ceased to run. The last of the belated sojourners had tramped his way up the carpeted stairs. On the fifth floor, as on all the others, a complete and absolute silence reigned. Suddenly a door was softly opened. Virginia, dressed in a loose gown, and wearing felt slippers which sank noiselessly into the thick carpet, came slowly out from her room. She looked all around and realized the complete solitude of the place. Then she crossed the corridor swiftly, and without a moment's hesitation fitted the key which she was carrying in her hand into the lock of Norris Vine's room. The door opened noiselessly. She closed it behind her and paused to listen. There was not a sound in the place, and the door on the left, which led into the sitting-room, was ajar. She stepped in, and, after another moment's hesitation, closed the door softly behind her and gently raised the blind. The sunlight came streaming in. There was no need for the electric light. The sitting room, none too tidy, showed signs of its owner's late return. There was a silk hat and a pair of white kid gloves upon the table, and on the sideboard a half-empty glass of whiskey and soda. Several cigarette ends were in the grate. An evening paper lay upon the hearthrug. She knew from these things that a few yards away Norris Vine lay sleeping.

Without hesitation, with swift and stealthy fingers, she commenced a close and careful scrutiny of every inch of the room. In a quarter of an hour she had satisfied herself. There was no hiding-place left which could possibly have escaped her. The more dangerous part of her enterprise was to come. Very softly she opened the door, leaving it ajar as she had found it. She stood before the closed door of the bedroom. Very slowly, and with the tips of her fingers, she turned the handle. It opened without a sound. She had no garments on that rustled, and the soles of her slippers were of thick felt. She stood inside the room without having made the slightest sound. She held her breath for a moment, and then summoning up her courage, she looked toward the bed. The close-drawn curtains were unable to altogether exclude the early morning sunlight which streamed in through the chinks of the curtains and the uncovered part of the window.

Virginia stood as though she had been turned to stone. Every nerve in her body seemed tense and quivering. The cry which rose from her heart parted her death-white lips, but remained unuttered. Wider and wider grew her eyes as she gazed with horror across the room. The power of action seemed to be denied to her. Her knees shook; a sort of paralysis seemed to stifle every sense of movement. She swayed and nearly fell, but her hand met the corner of the mantelpiece and she held herself erect. Gradually, second by second, the arrested life commenced to flow once more through her veins. She had but one impulse—to fly. She thought nothing of the motive of her coming, only to place the door between her and this! Unsteadily, but without accident, she passed through the door, and though her hand shook like a leaf, she managed to close it noiselessly again. Somehow, she never quite knew how, she found herself outside in the corridor, and a moment later safe in her own room with the door bolted. Then she threw herself upon the bed, and it seemed to her afterwards that she must have fainted!

* * * * *

Only a few hours later Guy, who had slept little that night, and had waked with a desperate resolve, stepped out of the lift and knocked at Virginia's door. There was no answer. The waiter came out from the service-room and approached him.

"The young lady has left, sir," he announced.

"Left?" Guy repeated aimlessly. "When? How long ago?"

"Barely half an hour, sir," the man answered.

"She paid up her bill as I know, and left the key behind. The rooms belong to her for another fortnight, but she didn't seem as though she were coming back."

"Did she leave any address for letters?" Guy asked.

"If you inquire at the office, sir, they will tell you," the man answered.

Guy went down to the office.

"Can you tell me," he asked, "if Miss Longworth has left any address?"

The man shook his head.

"She left an hour ago, sir," he said. "She said there would be no letters, and if we liked we could let her rooms, as she was certain not to come back."

"You cannot help me to find her, then?" Guy asked. "I am the Duke of Mowbray, and I should be exceedingly obliged to any one who could help me to discover this young lady."

They were all sent for at once, porter, commissionaire, hall-boy. The information he was able to obtain, however, was scanty indeed. Virginia had simply told the cabman, who had taken her and her luggage away, to drive along the Strand toward Charing Cross.

Guy drove back to Grosvenor Square, and insisted upon going up to his aunt's room. She received him under protest in her dressing-gown.

"My dear Guy," she expostulated, "what is the meaning of this? You know that I am never visible until luncheon time."

"Forgive me?" he said. "I scarcely know what I am doing this morning."

"Well, what is it?" she demanded.

"Virginia has gone!" he answered, "left her rooms, left no address behind her. What a fool I was not to follow her up last night! She waited until this morning. She must have expected that I would come, and I didn't. I was a d— —d silly ass!"

Lady Medlincourt yawned.

"Have you come here to tell me that, my dear Guy?" she said. "So unnecessary! You might at least have telephoned it."

"Look here," he said, "we were too rough on her yesterday afternoon. I made no conditions as to what she should tell me when I asked her to be my wife. I was quite content that she should say yes. I know she's all right; I feel it, and she's the only girl I shall ever care a fig for!"

"I really cannot see," Lady Medlincourt murmured, "why you should drag me from my bed to talk such rubbish. If you feel like that, go and look for her. It is open for you to marry whom you choose, the lady who is selling primroses at the corner of the Square if you wish. The only thing is that you cannot expect your friends to marry her too. What did you come here for, advice or sympathy? I have none of the latter for you, and you wouldn't take the former. Do, there's a good boy, leave me! I want to have my bath, and the hairdresser is waiting."

Guy turned on his heel and left the house. There was only one thing left to be done, although he hated doing it. He went to the office of a private detective.

"Mind," he said, when he had told them what he wanted, "I will not have the young lady worried or annoyed in any form if you should happen to find her. Simply let me know where she is living. The rest is my affair. You understand?"

"Perfectly!" the man answered. "We are to spare no expense, I presume?"

It did him good to be able to answer fervently, "None whatever, only find her!"

CHAPTER XV.
MR. DUGE THREATENS

The morning papers were full of the news. Phineas Duge had landed in London! The Stock Exchange was fluttered. Those whose hands were upon the money-markets of the world paused to turn their heads towards the hotel where he had taken a suite of rooms. Interviewers, acquaintances, actual and imaginary, beggars for themselves and for others, left their cards and hung around. In the hotel they spoke of him with bated breath, as though something of divinity attached itself to the person of the man whose power for good or for evil was so far-reaching.

Meanwhile Phineas Duge, who had had a tiresome voyage, and who was not a little fatigued, slept during the greater part of the morning following his arrival, with his faithful valet encamped outside the door. The first guest to be admitted, when at last he chose to rise, was Littleson. It was close upon luncheon time, and the two men descended together to the grillroom of the hotel.

"A quiet luncheon and a quiet corner," Littleson suggested, "some place where we can talk. Duge, it's good to see you in London. I feel somehow that with you on the spot we are safe."

Phineas Duge smiled a little dubiously. They found their retired corner and ordered luncheon. Then Littleson leaned across the table.

"Duge," he said, "I'm thankful that we've made it up. Weiss cabled me that you had come to terms, and that you were on your way over here to deal with the other matter. It's cost us a few millions to try and get the blind side of you."

Phineas Duge smiled very slightly; that is to say, his lips parted, but there was no relaxation of his features.

"Littleson," he said, "before we commence to talk, have you seen anything of my niece over here?"

Littleson was a little surprised. He had not imagined that Phineas Duge would ever again remember his niece's existence.

"Yes," he answered, "I crossed over with her."

"And since then?"

"I have seen her once or twice," Littleson answered a little dubiously.

"Alone?" Phineas Duge asked.

"Not always," Littleson answered. "Twice I have seen her with Norris Vine, and twice with a young Englishman who was on the steamer."

Phineas Duge said nothing for a moment. He seemed to be studying the menu, but he laid it down a little abruptly.

"Do you happen to know," he asked, "where she is now?"

"I haven't an idea," Littleson answered truthfully. "To be frank with you, she was not particularly amiable when I spoke to her on the steamer. She evidently wanted to have very little to say to me, so I thought it best to leave her alone."

"How long is it," Phineas Duge asked, "since you saw her?"

"It is about a week ago," Littleson answered. "She was dining at Luigi's with Norris Vine. I remember that I was rather surprised to see her with him. He seems to possess some sort of attraction for your family." Phineas Duge looked at the speaker coldly, and Littleson felt that somehow, somewhere, he had blundered. He made a great show of commencing his first course.

"Let me know exactly," Phineas Duge said, a moment or two later, "what you have done with regard to the man Vine."

Littleson glanced cautiously around.

"I have seen him," he said. "I have argued the matter from every possible side. I found him, I must say, absolutely impossible. He will not deal with us upon any terms. I fear that he is only biding his time. Every day I see by the papers that the agitation increases, and it seems to me that if this bill passes, we shall all practically be criminals. I think that Norris Vine is waiting for the moment when he can do so with the greatest dramatic effect, to fill his rotten paper with a verbatim copy of that document."

"It would be," Phineas Duge remarked,

"uncommonly awkward for you and Weiss and the others."

"We couldn't be extradited," Littleson answered, "and I shall take remarkably good care not to cross the ocean again until this thing has blown over."

"If it ever does," Phineas Duge remarked quietly. "Well, go on about Norris Vine."

Once more Littleson looked around the room.

"You know Dan Prince is over here?" he said softly.

Duge nodded.

"So far," he remarked, "his being over here does not seem to have affected the situation."

"He has made one attempt," Littleson whispered. "He got inside, and he had certain information that Vine was going to return that night. Whether he had warning or not no one can tell, but he never came back. They followed him a few nights ago across Trafalgar Square, hoping that he was going down toward the Embankment, but he took a hansom and drove to his club. They followed, and waited for him to come out, but there was a policeman standing at the very entrance, within a foot of them. This isn't New York, Duge. You can't depend upon getting the coast clear for this sort of thing over here, and Prince will take no risks. He is a rich man in his way, and he wants to live to enjoy his money. He's as clever as they make them, although he's failed twice here. I fancy he has something else pending."

"And meanwhile," Duge said quietly, "to-morrow morning's paper may contain our damnation."

"It may, of course," Littleson answered. "I don't think so, though. He doesn't move a yard without being shadowed, and he hasn't written out a cable when some one hasn't been near his shoulder."

"That is the position, then, so far as you know it?" Duge asked. "Absolutely!" Littleson answered. "I can tell you nothing more."

Duge finished his luncheon and signed the bill. Then he made an appointment to dine with Littleson, and sent out for an automobile. When it arrived he was driven to the American Embassy. At the mention of his name everything was made easy, and he found himself in a few minutes in the presence of the ambassador.

"Glad to meet you once more, Mr. Duge," he said. "You have forgotten me, I dare say, but I think we came across one another at a banquet in New York about four years ago."

"I remember it perfectly," Phineas Duge answered. "A dull affair it was, but we talked of the Asiatic Powers and kept ourselves amused. Since then, you see, all that I said has become justified."

Deane smiled.

"They say that with you that is always the case," he answered. "'Duge the Infallible' I heard a stockbroker once call you."

Duge smiled.

"Well," he said, "if I remember your politics, and I think I do, you are going to try and take away that title from me. You are amongst those, are you not, who have set themselves to dam the torrents?"

Deane shook his head a little stiffly.

"In the diplomatic service," he said, "we have no politics."

"Sometimes," Duge murmured, "you come in touch with them. For instance, I should like to know what advice you are going to give Norris Vine about the publication of that little document in his paper."

Deane looked for a moment annoyed.

"I am afraid," he said, "that I cannot answer you that question."

"If you advise him one way or the other," Phineas Duge said, "you give the lie to your own statement, that in diplomacy there are no politics. Your advice will show on which side you intend to stand."

"I have not given any advice," Deane replied.

"Nor must you," Phineas Duge said pleasantly enough. "It is not your affair at all, Mr. Deane. I grant your cleverness, your shrewdness, even your common sense, but all three are academic. They have no direct relation to the actual things of the world. Wealth is one of those forces which only strong fingers can gather, a stream which if you like you can divert, but you cannot dam. I want to tell you, Mr. Deane, that if you advise Norris Vine at all, you must see to it that you advise him to place that paper upon the fire, or to restore it from whence it was stolen."

"I am afraid, Mr. Duge," the ambassador said, "that I cannot recognize you as possessed of such authority as to justify the use of the word 'must.' I am in the habit of doing what I think right and well."

Phineas Duge bowed his head.

"I will only remind you, Mr. Deane," he said, "of the facts which led to the withdrawal of our ministers from Lisbon and Paris and Vienna. I am not proud of the power which undoubtedly lies in the palm of my right hand. On the other hand, I should be foolish if I did not remind you of these things at a time like this. I only ask you to take up a passive attitude. You escape in that way all trouble, and if you fancy that the climate of Paris would suit you or Mrs. Deane better than London, it would be a matter of a few months only; but— you must not advise the other way!"

The ambassador was distinctly uneasy. Duge saw his embarrassment and hastened on.

"I ask you for no reply, Mr. Deane," he said; "not even for an expression of opinion. I have said all that I came to say. Apart from any question of self-interest, I can assure you, as a man who sees as clearly as his neighbours, that you could do no good, but much evil, by advising Norris Vine to hold up these men to the ridicule and contempt of the world. He might sell a million copies of his paper, but he would create an enmity which in the end, I think, would swamp him. Mrs. Deane, I trust, is well?"

"She is in excellent health," the ambassador answered. "What can I do for you during your stay? I presume you know that anything you desire is open to you? You represent, you see, a great uncrowned royalty, to whom all the world bows. Will you come to Court?"

"Not I," Duge answered. "Those things are for another type of man. There was a further question which I wished to ask you. I have a niece who came over here on a foolish errand, a Miss Virginia Longworth. Do you happen to have seen or heard anything of her?"

"Nothing," the ambassador replied; "nothing personally, at any rate. I will inquire of my secretaries."

He left the room for a few minutes, and returned shaking his head.

"Nothing is known about her at all," he declared.

"If she should apply here," Duge said, rising and drawing on his gloves, "assist her in any way and let me know at once. She must be getting," he continued, "rather short of money. You can advance her whatever sum she asks for, and I will make it good."

Phineas Duge walked out into the sunlight and drove away in his automobile. Was it the glaring light, he wondered, the perfume of the flowers, the evidences on every side of an easier and less strenuous life, which were accountable for a certain depression, a slackening of interests which certainly seemed to come over him that afternoon as he drove back to the hotel. If he could have summarized his thoughts afterwards, he would have scoffed at them, as a grown man might laugh at a toy which a lunatic had offered him. Yet it is certain that the empty place by his side was filled more than once during that brief ride. He looked into the faces of the women and girls who streamed along the pavements with a certain half-eager curiosity, as though he expected to find a familiar face amongst them, a pale oval face, with quivering lips and lustrous appealing eyes—eyes which had come into his thoughts more often lately than he would have cared to admit.

"It is that infernal voyage!" he said to himself, as he got out of the car and entered the hotel. "One cannot think about reasonable things on days when the marconigram fails."

He bought a cigar at the stall and strolled over to the tape. It was a busy afternoon, and reports from America were coming in fast. He nodded as he turned away. Weiss and the rest had had their lesson. They were keeping, at any rate, to their part of the bargain.

CHAPTER XVI.
TRAPPED

Phineas Duge carefully drew off his gloves and laid them inside his hat. He declined a chair, however, and stood facing the man whom he had come to visit.

"I scarcely understand, Mr. Duge," Vine said, "what you can possibly want with me. Our former relations have scarcely been of so pleasant a nature as to render a visit from you easily to be understood."

"I will admit," Phineas Duge said coldly, "that personally I have no interest or any concern in you. But nevertheless there are two matters which must bring us together so far as the holding of a few minutes' conversation can count. In the first place, I want to know whether you are going to make use of the paper which my daughter stole, and which you feloniously received? In the second place, I want to know how much or what you will accept for the return of that paper? And thirdly, I want to know what the devil you have done with my niece, Virginia Longworth?"

"Your niece, Virginia Longworth," Norris Vine repeated thoughtfully.

"Are you in earnest, sir?"

"I am in earnest," Duge answered.

"Then I have done nothing with her," Vine declared. "I do not know where she is. I do not know why you should ask me?"

"You lie!" Phineas Duge said quietly. "But let that go. It is your trade, of course. I came here to give you the opportunity of answering questions. I scarcely expected that such direct methods would appeal to you."

"Your methods, at any rate," Vine said, moving toward the bell, "are not such as I am disposed to permit in my own apartment."

Phineas Duge stretched out his hand.

"One moment, Mr. Vine," he said.

Vine stopped.

"Well?" he asked.

"I refer again," Phineas Duge said, "to the question of my niece. As regards those other matters, if you do not wish to discuss them with me, let them go. Even in this country you will find that I am not powerless. But as regards my niece, I insist upon some explanation from you."

"Some explanation of what?" Vine asked.

"When she left New York a few months ago," Phineas Duge continued, "you and she were strangers. Granted that she came upon a silly errand, still it was not wholly her own fault, and she was only a simple child who ought never to have been permitted to have left America,"

"Up to that point, Mr. Duge," Vine said drily, "I am entirely in accord with you."

"She made your acquaintance somehow," Phineas Duge continued, "and you were seen out with her at different restaurants; once, I believe, at a place of amusement. She left her boarding-house and took rooms here in this building. Her room, I find, was across the corridor, only a few feet away from yours. What is there between you and my niece, Norris Vine?"

Vine leaned against the table, and a faint smile flickered over his face.

"Really, Mr. Duge," he said, "you must forgive my amusement. The idea that anything so trivial as the well-being of a niece should interest you in the slightest, seems to me almost paradoxical."

Phineas Duge was silent for several moments, his keen eyes fixed upon Vine's face.

"Pray enjoy your jests as much as you will, Mr. Vine," he said, "but answer my questions."

"Your niece," Norris Vine said, "came over here to rob me, at whose instigation I can only surmise. My first introduction to her was in my room, where she came as a thief. What consideration have you ever shown, Phineas Duge, even to the innocent who have crossed your paths? Why should you expect that I should show consideration to this simple child who came across the ocean to steal from me?"

There was still no change in Duge's face, but a little breath came quickly through his teeth, and, as though insensibly, he moved a little nearer to the man opposite him.

"Where is she now, Norris Vine?" he asked.

"If she is not in her rooms," Vine answered, "I do not know."

"She has given up her rooms, taken her luggage, and gone away," Duge said. "Perhaps it is you who have driven her out of this place."

"I was not aware of it," Vine answered. "As a matter of fact I expected her to lunch with me to-day."

Phineas Duge looked down upon the table before which he stood. He seemed to be turning something over in his mind, and opposite to him Norris Vine waited. When Duge looked up again, Vine seemed to notice for the first time that his visitor was aging.

"Norris Vine," he said, "you and I have been enemies since the day when we became aware of one another's existence. We represent different principles. There is not a point in life on which our interests, as well as our theories, do not clash. But there are things outside the battle for mere existence which men with any fundamental sense of honour can discuss, even though they are enemies. I wish to ask you once more whether you can give me any news of my niece."

"I can give you none," Norris Vine answered. "All that I can tell you is that I found her a charming, simple-minded girl, in terrible trouble because of your anger, and the fear that you would impoverish her people; and goaded on by that fear to attempt things which, in her saner moments, she would never have dreamed of thinking of. Where she is now, what has become of her, I do not know; but I would not like to be the person on whom rests the responsibility of her presence here and anything that may happen to her."

Phineas Duge took up his hat and gloves.

"I thank you, Mr. Vine," he said. "Your expression of opinion is interesting to me. In the meantime, to revert to business, am I right in concluding that you have nothing to say to me, that you do not wish even to discuss a certain matter?"

"You are right in your assumption, sir," Norris Vine answered. "I see no purpose in it. What I may do or leave undone would never be influenced by anything that you might say."

Phineas Duge turned toward the door. Norris Vine followed him. There was not, however, any motion on the part of either to indulge in any form of leave-taking; but Phineas Duge half opened the door, stood for a moment with his hand upon the handle, and looked back into the room.

"I fear, Mr. Vine," he said, "that you are developing an insular weakness. You are forgetting to be candid, and you are just a little too self-reliant."

He opened the door suddenly quite wide, but he made no motion to depart. On the contrary two men, who must have been standing within a foot or so of it, stepped quickly in. Phineas Duge closed the door.

CHAPTER XVII.
MR. DUGE FAILS

Norris Vine without a doubt was trapped. He realized it from the moment Phineas Duge closed the door and turned the key. The two men who had entered were to all appearance absolutely harmless and ordinary. They were dressed most correctly in dark clothes of fashionable cut. Each wore a silk hat, and would have passed without a moment's question amongst any ordinary group of better-class city men. Nevertheless, when at his quick motion toward the bell the fingers of one of them closed upon his arm, he knew very well that he was helpless. He suffered them to lead him without resistance into the little sitting-room. What could he have done? If he had opened his mouth to call out, he saw the hand of the man who was watching him, with his arm linked through his, ready to close his lips. They all passed into the sitting-room, and Phineas Duge closed the door behind them.

"I am sorry," he said, "to resort to such old-fashioned measures, but as you know I am methodical in all my ways. The first place to look for stolen goods is obviously in the abode of the thief. Frankly, I have not much expectation of discovering anything here. At the same time I could not afford to run the risk of leaving these rooms and your person unsearched."

"I can quite appreciate that," Norris Vine said, seating himself in the armchair towards which he was being gently pushed. "The only favour I will ask is that you are as quick as possible, as I have rather a busy afternoon, and want to lunch early."

"These gentlemen," Phineas Duge remarked, "are quite used to little affairs of this sort. I do not think that you need fear that there will be any undue delay."

Even while he spoke both of them were busy. Vine felt a silken cord being drawn about his legs and chest. Something was slid softly into his mouth. In less than two minutes he was bound and gagged. Then he had an opportunity, so far as the sitting-room was concerned, of watching a search conducted upon scientific principles.

In about twenty minutes the place looked as though a tornado had struck it. The search, however, was over. The two men were prepared to guarantee that no papers of any sort were hidden in any place within the reach of any one in that room. They carried him, bound as he was, into the bedroom, and he watched with interest, and some admiration, a repetition of the search. The result, however, was the same. Then the two men came over to him, and he felt his bonds softly loosened. Only the gag remained in his mouth, and one by one his garments were removed from him. A trained valet could not have been more careful or deft. The contents of all his pockets were hastily run through and restored. His under garments were felt all over for any hidden hiding place. Even his shoes were taken off, and the inner sole cut through with a knife. Finally the two men turned towards Phineas Duge. Their faces were a mute expression of the fact that the search was over. Phineas Duge motioned them to remove the gag. They did so, and Vine, who was now free, stood up and commenced to dress.

"I am sorry," Phineas Duge said calmly, "to have inconvenienced you, but, of course, a person who becomes a receiver of stolen goods is always liable to a little affair of this sort. You are quite at liberty to ring the bell now if you like, and to make complaints about us. My methods may have seemed to you a little melodramatic, but as a matter of fact they are entirely commonplace. These two gentlemen are connected with the American police, and it may interest you to know that we have with us warrants for the arrest both of yourself and my daughter, Miss Stella Duge, on the charge of theft and conspiracy. All that we have done here has been quite legal, except that we should have been accompanied by a gentleman from Scotland Yard, with whose presence we preferred to dispense. You can make what complaints you like, and I shall immediately apply for your extradition. In any case I expect to do so to-morrow or the next day, if a certain document is not forthcoming. You see I am placing myself in your hands. You have time even now to cable its contents to New York before the warrant can be executed."

Norris Vine was busy tying his tie, and waited for a moment until he had arranged it to his satisfaction. Then he turned round.

"I can assure you," he said, "I had not the slightest intention of making any complaint with regard to your doings here. In fact, I can truthfully say that I have rather enjoyed the whole proceeding. To tell you the truth," he continued, moving across the room and taking a cigarette from the mantelpiece and lighting it, "when I heard that you were in England, I was exceedingly curious to know what your methods would be. 'Phineas Duge the Invincible' they have called you. I knew that you came over here because you had entered in a fresh alliance with your gang, and I knew therefore that you came over to get back that document. I imagine that if you can get it you can make your own terms with them. I must say that I have been exceedingly curious to know what your methods would be in approaching me. Littleson could suggest nothing better than a bribe and a common burglary. There is something much more attractive about the way you have opened the proceedings. I consider that this little affair, for instance, has been most artistic. If you have not discovered what you sought, you have at least discovered the fact that it is not here. That gives you something to start upon. How kind of your assistants! I see that they are putting my room straight again."

Phineas Duge nodded. He showed no disappointment at the ill-success of this first effort, and he was watching Vine all the time curiously.

"Your further plan of operations," Vine continued, "is again worthy of you. I believe all that you say. I believe that you have the warrants, and I believe that you could easily obtain an extradition order. On the other hand, I am perfectly well aware that this is only a feint. It is a good scheme up to a certain point, of course, although neither your daughter nor myself could be convicted of conspiracy without the production of what we are supposed to have stolen. Still, as I said, it is a good feint, and it has made me curious. I wonder what your real scheme is! I do not think that you will tell me that."

Phineas Duge smiled.

"You should have been a diplomatist. Mr. Vine," he said. "As a journalist you are wasted. You might even have achieved what I presume you would have called infamy, as a financier."

"Ah, well!" Norris Vine said, "the world is full of those who have missed their vocation. I am content to pass amongst the throng. Can I offer you anything before you go? A whisky and soda, or a glass of sherry?"

"I think not, thank you," Phineas Duge said. "You are naturally in a hurry to keep your luncheon engagement, and I see that my friends have succeeded in restoring your apartment to some semblance of order. We part now to pass on to the second stage of our little duel. Understand that, so far as regards this little matter of business, I have no special ill-feeling towards you, Mr. Vine. I ask you even no questions concerning your friendship with my daughter. She is old enough to know her own mind, and she has heard my views often enough; but I should like you to know this, and to remember that I who say it am a man of many faults, but one virtue: never in my life have I broken my word. If I find that my niece has disappeared through any ill-usage of yours, I will risk the few years that may be left to me of life, and I will shoot you like a dog the first time that we meet."

Norris Vine looked gravely across at the man whose words so quietly spoken, seemed yet from their very repression to be charged with an intense dramatic force. He knew so well that the man who spoke them meant what he said and would surely keep his word. He shrugged his shoulders very slightly.

"My dear sir," he said, "I fear that I have misunderstood you. I could have imagined your sentiment being aroused by the sight of a dollar bill being burnt and wasted, but I never expected to see it kindled upon the subject of your niece, or any other human being. I amend my judgment of you. You are really not the man I thought you were. If your friends have quite finished "—he took up his hat and glanced for a moment at his watch. Duge turned toward the door.

"Once more, Mr. Vine," he said, "my regrets, and good morning!"

The three men left the room. Vine remained, leaning against the mantelpiece, and whistling softly to himself. He went through the whole of a popular ballad, and then he tried it in a different key. When he was sure that the three men had had time to leave the building, he too took up his hat and went out.

CHAPTER XVIII.
ADVICE FOR MR. VINE

Mr. Deane was on the point of accompanying his wife for their usual afternoon's drive in the park. A glance at the card which was brought to him just as he was preparing to leave the house, however, was sufficient to change his plans.

"My dear," he said to his wife, "you will have to excuse me this afternoon. I have a caller whom I must see."

"Shall I wait for a few minutes?" she asked.

"Better not," he answered, "I imagine that I may be detained some time."

He took off his hat and coat, and made his way to the library, where Phineas Duge was awaiting him. The ambassador was a broad-minded man, loath to take sides unless he was compelled in the huge struggle, the coming of which he had prophesied years ago. He recognized in Phineas Duge one of the great powers at the back of the nation which he represented, and as a diplomatist he was fully prepared to receive him, and welcome him as one.

"I am very glad to see you again, Mr. Duge," he said, hospitably, extending his hand, "I hope that you have changed your mind, and are going to let us put you in the way of a few social amusements while you are over here."

"You are very kind," Duge answered, "but I think not. My visit here has to do with two matters only, to both of which I think I have already referred. You have heard nothing of my niece?"

"Nothing whatever, I am sorry to say," Mr. Deane answered.

"Well, there remains the other matter," Duge answered. "You and I have already had a few words concerning that, and I am pleased to see that up to the present, at any rate, our friend Mr. Vine has been governed by the dictates of common sense. Still, I think you can understand that so long as that paper exists the situation is an unpleasant one."

Mr. Deane inclined his head slowly.

"Without a doubt," he admitted, "it would be more comfortable for you and your friends to feel that the document in question was no longer in existence."

"I am here in the interests," Mr. Duge answered a little stiffly, "of my friends only. My own name does not appear upon it. However, my anxiety to discover its whereabouts is none the less real."

"You have seen Mr. Vine?" Mr. Dean asked.

"I have," Duge answered, "and I have come to the conclusion, for which I have some grounds, that the document is not for the moment in his possession. I have therefore asked myself the question—to whom on this side would he be likely to entrust it? It occurred to me that it might be deposited at a bank, but I find that he has no banking account over here. The American Express Company have no packet in their charge consigned by him. Therefore I have come to the conclusion that he has placed it in the care of some friend in whom he has unlimited confidence. Foolish thing that to have, Mr. Deane," Phineas Duge continued slowly, with his eyes fixed upon his companion. "One is likely to be deceived even by the most unlikely people."

"Your business career," Mr. Deane replied courteously, "no doubt has taught you that caution is next to genius."

"I would have you," Phineas Duge said impressively, "lay that little axiom of yours to heart, Mr. Deane. I think you will agree with me that a man in your position especially, the accredited ambassador of a great country, should show himself more than ordinarily cautious in all his doings and sayings, especially where the interests of any portion of his country people are concerned."

"I trust, Mr. Duge," the ambassador replied, "that I have always realized that."

"I too hope so," Duge answered. "I told you, I think, that I had come to the conclusion that Norris Vine, not having that paper any longer in his possession, has passed it on to some other person in whom his faith is unbounded."

"You did, I believe, mention that supposition," Mr. Deane assented.

"I ask myself, therefore," Phineas Duge continued, "who, amongst his friends in London, Norris Vine would be most likely to trust with the possession of a document of such vast importance. Need I tell you the first idea which suggested itself to me! It is for your advice that Norris Vine has crossed the ocean. You have read the document. You know its importance. There would, I imagine, be no hiding place in London so secure as the Embassy safe which I see in the corner of your study!"

"You suggest, then," Mr. Deane said slowly, "that Norris Vine has deposited that document in my keeping."

"I not only suggest it," Duge answered, "but I am thoroughly convinced that such is the fact. Can you deny it?"

Mr. Deane shrugged his shoulders.

"The matter, so far as I am concerned in it," he answered, "is a personal one between Vine and myself. I cannot answer your question."

Phineas Duge shook his head thoughtfully.

"That, Mr. Deane," he said, "is where you make a great mistake. Permit me to say that your official position should, I am sure, preclude you from taking any part in this business. The matter, you say, is a private one. There can be no private matters between you, the paid and accredited agent of your country, and one of its citizens. To speak plainly, you have not the right to offer the shelter of the Embassy to the document which Norris Vine has committed to your charge."

"How do you know that he has done so?" Deane asked.

"Call it inspiration if you like," Duge answered. "In any case I am sure of it."

There was a short silence. Then Mr. Deane rose to his feet a little stiffly.

"Perhaps you are right," he said, "and yet I am not sure."

"A little reflection will, I think, convince you," Phineas Duge said quietly. "Your retention of that document means that you take sides in the civil war which seems hanging over my country. Further than that, it also means—and although it pains me to say so, Mr. Deane, I assure I you say it without any ill-feeling—a serious interruption to your career."

The ambassador was silent for several moments.

"Mr. Duge," he said, "I am inclined to admit that up to a certain point you have reason on your side. It is true that I am guarding the document in question for Norris Vine, and it is also true that in doing so I am perhaps departing a little from the strict propriety which my position demands. I will therefore return to him the document, but I should like you to understand that with every desire to retain your good will, I shall give Mr. Vine such advice with regard to the use of it as seems to me, as a private individual and a citizen of the United States, judicious."

Phineas Duge took up his hat.

"As to that," he said, "I have nothing to say, beyond this. However things may shape themselves in the immediate future, my influence will, I believe, still prove something to be reckoned with on the other side. That influence, Mr. Deane, I use for those who show themselves my friends."

The two men parted with some restraint. Deane, after a few minutes' hesitation, went to the telephone and called up Vine at his club.

"I want to talk to you, Vine, at once," he said. "Can you come round?"

"In ten minutes," was the answer.

"I shall wait for you," the ambassador answered, ringing off.

CHAPTER XIX.
THE CRISIS

In a small, shabbily furnished room at the top of a tall apartment house, Virginia was living through what seemed to her, as indeed it was, a grim little tragedy. On the table before her was her little purse, turned inside out, and by its side a few, a very few coins. The roll of notes, which she had not changed, and which formed the larger part of her little capital, was gone, hopelessly, absolutely gone. It was nothing less than a disaster this, which she was forced to face. She had left the purse about in her rooms in Coniston Mansions, or there were many other places in which an expert thief would have found it a very easy matter to remove the little bundle and replace it with that roll of paper which she found in its place.

Her first wild thought of rushing to the police-station she had dismissed as useless. She had no idea when or where the theft had been accomplished; only she knew that she was alone in a strange city, and that the few shillings left to her were not even sufficient to pay for the rent she already owed for her room.

She dragged herself to the window and stood looking out across the grimy house-tops. Her eyes were blurred with tears. It is doubtful whether she saw anything of the uninspiring view, but it seemed to her that she could certainly see the wreck of her own short life. She seemed to realize then the mad folly of her journey, the hopelessness of it from beginning to end. Quite apart from her failure, there was also a madness of which she refused even to think, the aftertaste of those few hours of delicious happiness. Had he ever tried to find her out, she wondered, since that day when she had fled with burning cheeks and aching heart from her rooms in Coniston Mansions, and sought to hide herself in the cold bosom of this unlovely city. In any case she would never see him again. Her one desire now, if it amounted to a desire, when all ways in life seemed to her alike flat and profitless, was to find her way somehow or other back to America, and to carry the bad news herself to the little farmhouse in the valley.

She looked at her pitiful little store of coins, and the problem of existence seemed to become more and more difficult. After all, there was another way for those who did not care to live. She found herself harbouring the thought without a single sign of any revulsion of feeling, accepting it as a matter to be seriously considered with dull, calculating fatalism. What was the use of life when nothing remained to hope for! It was, after all, an easy way out.

She opened the window and looked below. The seven stories made her dizzy. Nevertheless, she looked with a curious fascination to the stone courtyard immediately underneath the window. Death would probably be instantaneous. She leaned a little further out and then started suddenly back into the room. A revulsion of feeling had overtaken her. It was a hideous idea, this. For the sake of the others she must put it away from her. She walked up and down the narrow confines of her room, and then the necessity for action of some sort drove her out into the street. Curiously enough, though she was being searched for by at least half a dozen detectives and inquiry agents, she had taken no particular pains to conceal herself beyond the fact that she had chosen a crowded and low-class neighbourhood, and had seldom ventured out before dark. She walked now to the office of a shipping agent which she had noticed on her way here, and addressed herself to the clerk who hastened forward to ascertain her wishes.

"I want," she said, "to get to America, and have no money. All that I had has been stolen. Could I get a passage and pay for it when I arrive? A second class passage, of course."

The clerk shook his head dubiously.

"Have you no friends in London," he asked, "to whom you could apply for a loan?"

"Not a single one," she answered.

"Why not cable?" he suggested. "You could have money wired over here to your credit."

"I do not wish to do that," Virginia answered.

The young man shrugged his shoulders.

"The only other course," he said, "would be to apply to the Embassy. They might advance the money."

Virginia walked out thoughtfully. After all, why not? Mr. Deane, she knew, was a friend of her uncle's. He would perhaps let her have the money, and she could send it back later on. She walked to the great house in Ormande Gardens and asked to see Mr. Deane. The servant who admitted her hesitated a little.

"There is no one in just now, miss," he said, "except Mr. Deane, and he is busy with a gentleman. If you will come into the waiting-room, I will ask him whether he can spare you a moment when the gentleman has gone."

Virginia sat upon a very hard horsehair chair in a barely furnished room, and waited. The table was covered with magazines, but she did not touch them. She sat nervously twisting and untwisting her fingers. Then the sudden sound of voices outside attracted her attention. The door of the room in which she sat had been left ajar, and apparently two men, passing down the hall from a room on the other side, had paused just outside it.

"Of course, I don't know what you will do with it, Vine," she heard some one say, "but if you take my advice, you will find a secure hiding place without a moment's delay. I am very sorry indeed that I cannot help you out any longer, but I know you don't want me to run risks."

"Rather not," Vine answered. "To tell you the truth, I think my mind is made up. I am going to spend a little fortune cabling to-night."

"Well, I am not sure but that you are wise," was the reply. "It's one of those things the result of which it is quite impossible to prophesy. Good luck to you anyway, Vine, and do, for the next few hours, take care of yourself."

Then Virginia heard a parting between the two men. One of them apparently left the house, the other returned to the room from which they had issued. Virginia did not hesitate for a moment. She passed on tiptoe out of the room into the hall. A servant stood at the front door, having that moment let Vine out.

"I have decided not to wait for Mr. Deane any longer," she said. "I will call and see one of the secretaries sometime to-morrow."

The man let her out without question. She was just in time to see Vine turn the corner of the square. She followed him breathlessly, then paused and stopped a passing hansom.

"Coniston Mansions," she told the man. "Please go as quickly as you can."

She was driven there, and passed quickly through the hall and entered the lift. The commissionaire hurried up to her.

"Several people, miss, have been asking for your address since you left," he announced.

"I will leave it before I go," she answered hurriedly.

She got out at the fifth floor, and without hesitation she walked straight across to Norris Vine's rooms. She was as pale as death. After that last visit of hers she felt a horrible shrinking from entering the place. Nevertheless, she drew a key from her pocket, turned the lock, entered, and found, as she supposed, that she was there first. She looked around, at first in vain, for some hiding place. All the while she was struggling to put everything else out of her mind except two great facts. Norris Vine was going to bring that paper back to his rooms! It was her last chance! If she failed this time, there was nothing left for her but despair! On the right of the outside door was a small clothes cupboard. It was the only place in the two rooms where concealment seemed in any way possible, and Virginia, with beating heart, stepped into it and drew the door to after her. She was scarcely there before she heard the sound of a key in the lock. She drew back, holding her breath as he passed. Norris Vine entered and stepped into the sitting-room. She heard him take off his hat and coat and throw them down. She heard the sound of a chair drawn up to the table. He was preparing, then, to write out his cable!

CHAPTER XX.
BEWITCHED

Very softly Virginia pushed open the door one, two, three inches. She could see Vine now sitting at the table with several sheets of paper before him, and a book which seemed to be a code, the leaves of which he was turning over meditatively. Her eyes were fastened upon that roll of paper at his left-hand side. She had no doubt but that it was the document which had been stolen, the document to recover which had brought her upon this wild-goose chase. The very sight of it, even at this distance, thrilled her. Scheme after scheme rushed through her brain. There were overcoats hanging up in the closet. Could she steal out on tiptoe, throw one over his head, and escape with the paper before he could stop her? Even then, unless she had time to lock him in, what chance would she have of leaving the building?

She watched him write, without undue haste, but referring every now and then to the code-book by his side. If only he would get up and go into the bedroom for a moment, it might give her a chance. She could feel her heart beating underneath her gown. Every sense was thrilling with excitement; and then, all of a sudden, she had a great surprise. Almost a cry broke from her lips; almost she had taken that swift involuntary movement forward, for she realized suddenly that she was not the only one who was watching Norris Vine. Very softly a man, coatless and in his socks, had stolen out from the bedroom where he had lain concealed, and was looking in through the opening of the partly closed study door. Virginia felt her finger-nails dig into her flesh. She stood there rapt and breathless. Instinctively she felt that the cards had been taken from her hand, that she was to be a witness of events more swift and definite than any in which she herself could have borne the principal part.

Norris Vine was absorbed in his work. She saw him bend lower and lower over the table, and she heard his pen drive faster across the paper. His attention was riveted upon his task. She saw the man lurking behind the door come gradually more into evidence. He was a stranger to her, but she could see that he was an athlete by his broad shoulders, his long arms, and his graceful poise, as he lurked there almost like a tiger preparing for a spring. Of what his plan might be she could form no idea. Every pulse in her body was beating as it had never beat before. Her breath was coming sharply and quickly, and it was all that she could do to keep back the sobs which seemed to rise in her throat from pure excitement. What was he going to do, this man who crouched there, nerving himself as though for some great effort! Very soon she knew.

He stole to the limit of the protection afforded him by the door. She saw his head turn a little sideways, and she saw his eyes fixed upon a certain spot in the wall. Then he glanced back again toward the man writing, as though he measured the distance between them, as though he wished even to calculate the exact nature of the movement which it was necessary to make. Then in the midst of her wondering came the elucidation of these things. The man poised himself. She could see him in the act of springing. He made a dash, hit something with his hand, and the room was in darkness! She heard him leap across the room toward the table, and she heard the low cry of Norris Vine as he sprang to his feet to meet this unknown assailant. She knew very well in the darkness which way the struggle must go. Norris Vine, slim, a hater of exercise, unmuscular, unprepared, could have no chance against an attack like this.

Virginia's brain moved swiftly in those few moments. She heard the quick breath of the two men as they swayed in one another's arms, and she did not hesitate for a moment. On tiptoe, and with all the grace and lightness which were hers, by right of her buoyant figure and buoyant youth, she crossed the room with swift, silent footsteps, and gathered into her hands the roll of papers upon the table. As softly as she had come she went. The deep sobbing breaths of the two men, the half-stifled cries with which Vine was seeking for outside help, effectually deadened the faint swish of her skirts and the tremor of her footsteps upon the carpeted floor.

She came and went like a dream, and when the man, in whose arms Norris Vine was after all but a child, finally dragged his victim across the floor by the collar and turned up the electric light, the table towards which he looked was bare. He dropped Vine heavily upon the floor, and stood there rooted to the spot, gazing at the place where only a few moments before he had seen that roll of paper. A hoarse imprecation broke from his lips, and Norris Vine, who was still conscious though badly winded, seeing what was amiss, sat up on the carpet and gazed too, bewildered, at the empty table. The papers were gone! There was no sign of them there. There was no sign of any one else in the apartment. There was nothing to indicate that any one had entered it or left it. The man who had thought himself the victor stood there with his hands to his head, an unimaginative person, but suddenly dazed with a curious crowd of apprehensions. Norris Vine staggered up to his feet, and groped his way toward the sideboard, where a decanter of brandy was standing.

"Good God!" he muttered to himself, as he poured some of the liquor into a glass and raised it to his lips. "Are we all mad or bewitched or what?"

His assailant did not answer. He raised the table-cloth and looked underneath, retreated into the bedroom, sought in vain for any signs of an intruder. Then he came slowly back into the sitting-room, and the eyes of the two men met. Norris Vine was leaning back against the sideboard, his clothes disarranged, his collar torn, his tie hanging down in strips. In his shaking hand was the glass of brandy, half consumed. There was a livid mark upon his face, and his eyes were wide open and staring.

"My muscular friend," he said, "the ghosts have robbed you."

"Ghosts be d— —d!" the other man answered, a little wildly. "I wish this job were at the bottom of the ocean before I'd touched it."

CHAPTER XXI.
A LESSON LEARNED

The American ambassador was giving the third of his great dinner-parties. At the last moment he had prevailed upon Phineas Duge to accept an invitation. Littleson, also, was of the party, and the ladies having departed, these three, separated only by the German ambassador, who was engaged in an animated conversation with a Russian Grand Duke, found themselves for a minute or two detached from the rest of the party. Littleson took the opportunity to move his chair over until he was able to whisper into Duge's ear.

"Any news?"

"None!" Duge answered shortly.

Mr. Deane leaned forward in his chair.

"I suppose you have heard," he said, "that a warrant was issued this afternoon for the arrest of your friends, Higgins and Weiss?"

"It was a matter of form only," Duge replied.

"Unless they pass this new bill through the Senate, nothing more than a little temporary inconvenience can happen to them. I wonder why our great President has developed so sudden and violent an antipathy to capital."

"I am not sure," Mr. Deane replied, "whether his position is logical. Capital must be the backbone of any great country, and the very elements of human nature demand its concentration. I think myself that this will all blow over."

"Unless—" Littleson whispered.

"Unless," Mr. Deane continued, "some greater scandal than any at present known were to attach itself to our two friends."

"One cannot tell," Phineas Duge said slowly. "Such a scandal might come. It is hard to say. The ways that lead to great wealth are full of pitfalls, and they are not ways that stand very well the blinding glare of daylight."

Littleson was looking pale and nervous. He drew a little breath and fanned himself with his handkerchief.

"You men love to talk in riddles," he said, or rather whispered, hoarsely. "Why not admit that they are safe enough so long as Norris Vine does not move!"

A servant approached the ambassador and whispered in apologetic fashion in his ear.

"There is a young lady, sir," he said, "who has just arrived, and who insists upon seeing you. She says that her business is of the utmost importance. I have done my best to make her understand that you are engaged, but she will not listen to reason. She is, I think, sir, an American young lady, and she is very much disturbed."

Phineas Duge leaned forward in his place. His eyes were fixed upon the servant. He said nothing. He only waited.

"A young American lady!" Mr. Deane repeated slowly. "Have you seen her before?"

"I believe, sir," the man answered, "that it is the same young lady who came here some weeks ago to inquire after Mr. Norris Vine."

Phineas Duge was on his feet with a sudden soft, half-stifled exclamation. Mr. Deane looked around the table. His other guests were all talking amongst themselves. Littleson, ignorant of what this might mean, was looking a little bewildered. The ambassador addressed one of the men a little lower down the table.

"Sinclair," he said, "will you take my place for a moment? A little matter of business has turned up, and I am wanted. I shall not be away long."

The man addressed nodded, and, pushing back his chair, strolled toward the ambassador's vacant seat, his cigar in his mouth. Phineas Duge and Mr. Deane left the room together, and close behind them Littleson followed. They left the room without any appearance of haste, but once in the hall Phineas Duge showed signs of a rare impatience, and pushed his way on ahead. The door of the waiting-room was half open. He strode in, and a little exclamation broke from his lips. It was Virginia who stood there, and her hands were crossed upon her bosom, as though there were something there which she was guarding. Nevertheless, at the sight of her uncle they fell away, and she started back.

"You!" she exclaimed. "Uncle Phineas! Here in London!"

He saw the signs stamped into her face of the evil times through which she had passed, and the more immediate traces of the crisis which lay so close behind her. He held out both his hands, and stepped quickly toward her. He was only just in time to save her from falling.

"I came," she faltered, "to get money from Mr. Deane to send you a cable, to catch a steamer to come back to America. I have got it!" she cried suddenly, her voice rising almost to a hysterical shriek. "I have got it! It is here! See!"

She dragged something from the front of her dress—a roll of papers, and held them out. She was swaying upon her feet now, and Phineas Duge, his arm around her waist, half led, half carried her to a chair. Littleson, who had darted out of the room, came back with a glass of water. All three men stood around her. The papers were there upon her knee, but her fingers seemed wound around them with some unnatural force. Her burning eyes were fixed upon her uncle's.

"Take them!" she begged. "Read them! Tell me that it is all right. Tell me that you will keep your promise."

He took them gently away. A single glance at the sheet of foolscap was enough.

"You are a wonderful child, Virginia," he said calmly. "It is as you say. These are the papers which Stella stole. I blamed you for the loss of them too hardly, but you shall never be sorry that you succeeded in regaining them."

She drew a queer little breath of relief, and leaned back in her chair. She was still as pale as death, but the terrible strain had gone from her face.

"I snatched them up," she murmured, "and ran. I am sure they will come after me. And Vine—I think that that man will kill Vine. His fingers were upon his throat when I left."

"You brought them," Phineas Duge asked calmly, "from Norris Vine's rooms?"

She had no time to answer. The door was opened. Norris Vine stood there on the threshold. He looked in upon the little group and shrugged his shoulders.

"I am too late, then," he said slowly.

Phineas Duge thrust his hand into the flames and held the papers there. Norris Vine seemed for a moment as though he would have sprung forward, but Littleson intervened, and Deane himself.

"They shall burn!" Duge cried. "If you are really the altruist you claim to be, Mr. Vine, you need not fear their destruction. We are changing our tactics. If the bill becomes law we will face its effect, whatever it may be. There shall be no bribery. There shall be no underground history. If the people of America attack us, we will fight our own battles."

Norris Vine sighed.

"In another half an hour," he said, "my cable would have been sent. To-morrow New York would have been indeed the city of unrest."

Phineas Duge turned upon him coldly.

"You," he said, "are one of those unpractical persons, who bring to the affairs of a purely utilitarian epoch the 'fainéant' scruples of the dilettante and romanticist. You cannot regulate the flow of wealth any more than you can dam a river with shifting sand. Don't you know that destiny, whether it be guided by other powers or not, was never meant to be shaped by the lookers-on?"

Norris Vine shrugged his shoulders and turned toward the door.

"Well," he said, "I will not argue with you. Perhaps those papers are better where they are. You will learn your lesson. You, sir," he added, turning to Littleson, "and those other of your friends who, at any rate, have known the shadow of an American prison, in some other way."

CHAPTER XXII.
A SURPRISE

Norris Vine put on his coat, lit a cigarette, and looked around the room with the satisfied air of a man who has successfully accomplished a difficult task. In front of him were two steamer trunks, a hold-all, hat-box, a case of guns, golf clubs, and some smaller packages, all fastened up and labelled "Vine, New York." He moved toward the bell, meaning to ring for a porter, but was interrupted by a knock at the door.

"Come in!" he called out, and Virginia entered. He looked at her in cold surprise. He recognized her, of course, but he recognized also that this young lady had nothing whatever to do with the pale-faced, desperate child, whose visits to him before had always seemed in a sense pathetic. He was an artist in such things, and he realized at once the dainty perfection of her muslin gown and large drooping hat. Her whole expression, too, had changed. She had no longer the look of a hunted and frightened child. She carried herself with confidence and with colour in her cheeks, and though she held out her hand to him with some show of timidity, the smile upon her lips was delightful, if a little appealing. "Mr. Vine," she said, "please forgive my coming. I have something so important to say to you and I heard that you were going back to the States. You will spare me a few minutes, will you not?"

Vine was only human, and hers was an appeal it was not easy to refuse. He placed a chair for her, and stood in a listening attitude.

"My dear young lady," he said, "I will listen gladly to anything that you have to say. But as I have nothing more left which it would be of any interest to you to steal, I scarcely understand to what I am indebted for this unexpected"—he hesitated for a moment and concluded his sentence with a not ungracious bow—"unexpected pleasure!" he said.

She smiled up at him delightfully.

"I am so glad, Mr. Vine," she said, "that you are going to be generous and nice, because what I have to say to you is so difficult, and if you were angry with me it would be very hard to say."

"I trust," he answered, "that I can accept a defeat; and you had all the luck, you know."

"I had," she admitted. "It was, after all, nothing to do with me. I see you have cleared your cupboard out. I can assure you that it was a terribly stuffy place with all those clothes of yours hanging there."

He smiled.

"Well," he said, "you were very patient and very persistent. You have won and I lost. I am not at all sure that it is not a good thing that I lost. My friend Deane tells me so even now. But let that go. I am sure you would like to tell me what it is that you have come here for."

"I have come," she answered, "to talk to you about Stella."

"Stella?" he repeated slowly.

Virginia nodded.

"Yes!" she said. "You see, I have all the time the feeling that I have somehow or other done Stella an injury by taking her place with my uncle, and do you know, Mr. Vine, since he has been in London he seems quite altered. He has been simply delightful, and I haven't felt frightened by him once. He keeps on giving me beautiful presents, and he does not seem in the least in a hurry to get back to America."

Norris Vine smiled grimly.

"I do not blame him," he said.

"Yesterday," she continued, "I could not help it; I disobeyed his orders and I spoke to him about Stella, and do you know, he listened to me quite patiently. Mr. Vine, I am going to say something to you very serious. You must not ask me how I know, or exactly what I know; but I accidentally do know so much as this. You and Stella are very fond of one another, and I should like to see you married."

He raised his eyebrows slowly.

"You would like," he repeated, "to see us married!"

She looked away from him. He could see that for some reason or other she was embarrassed. The colour had streamed into her cheeks, but she went on bravely enough.

"Yes!" she said. "I talked to my uncle about it, and he was quite nice. He says that he does not want to see Stella again for a short time, but if you two have made up your minds to be married—that is how he put it—he is going to give Stella a million dollars."

"You must be a magician," he said coolly.

"I am nothing of the sort," she answered, "but I think that my uncle has been very much misunderstood, or else something has changed him wonderfully during the past few months. Now, I came straight to see you and to tell you this, Mr. Vine, because I do not know where to find Stella. Can't you be married here in London, and ask me to the wedding?"

There was a knock at the door and it was immediately opened. They both turned round. It was Stella who stood there. She looked at them both for a moment in surprise. Then she closed the door and came into the room.

"Virginia!" she exclaimed. "What on earth are you doing here?"

"I should have come to see you, Stella," Virginia said, "if I had known where to find you."

"Virginia has come," Vine said, "to tell us that your father is inclined to play the part of a benevolent parent. I think that he must be either very ill, or going to be. Virginia has come here to tell us that we are to be married, and that he is going to give you some little trifle for a wedding present, a million dollars, I think it was she mentioned."

Stella looked at her cousin in amazement.

"Do you mean this, Virginia?" she exclaimed.

"Absolutely," Virginia answered. "He has promised faithfully. There is no doubt about it at all."

"Thank goodness!" Stella declared. "I am tired of being poor, aren't you, Norris? Virginia, you're a dear."

Stella passed her arm around her cousin's neck. Virginia looked up a little timidly.

"And you will marry Mr. Vine, then," she said, "at once?"

Stella laughed softly.

"My dear child," she said, "we have been married for six weeks."

Virginia leaned back in her chair.

"Oh!" she said. Then suddenly she sprang to her feet. She was obviously delighted. A certain restraint had left her manner. It was clear that the news was a relief to her.

"This," she said, "is delightful. You are both of you to come to dinner to-night at Claridge's. Your father told me that I was to ask you," she said, turning to Stella, "if I found you both,"

"At eight o'clock, I suppose?" Vine remarked. "We will be there."

Virginia and Stella left together.

"I have an automobile outside," Virginia said a little shyly. "Your father is ever so much too kind to me, but I do hope, Stella, that you don't mind. I feel sure that he is going to be quite different now."

"Mind? Of course not," Stella answered. "I have been rather a beast to him myself, and I think it's very decent of you, after everything, to have anything to do with me. Who on earth is this young man?"

They were in the hall of the Mansions, face to face with a young man who was in the act of entering. Virginia looked up, and gave a startled little cry.

"You!" she exclaimed breathlessly.

Guy quite ignored her companion, and took her by the hands. "Virginia!" he exclaimed. "At last! Where have you been hiding yourself, and how dared you run away from me?"

"There didn't seem to be much else for me to do," Virginia answered smiling; "but I am very glad to see you again now," she added in a lower tone.

"How well you look!" he exclaimed. "Where can we go and sit down? I want to talk to you, and remember I am not going to let you out of my sight again."

Stella, whom they had both forgotten, intervened.

"It seems to me," she said, "that it is fortunate I have an engagement. At eight o'clock then, Virginia."

Guy lifted his hat, and Virginia murmured something.

"It is my cousin Stella," she said. "What is it that you want to say to me, Guy?" she added, half shyly, as soon as they were alone.

"Come and get in my automobile," he said. "We will sit behind and let the man drive. Then we can talk. But the first thing I have to say to you is this: that I do not want to ask you a single question, nor am I going to permit any one else to ask you anything. Whoever you are and whatever you are, you are going to be my wife as soon as I can get another special license."

She laughed softly.

"Very well," she said, "only you must come in my automobile instead, and send yours away. If you like I will take you for a little drive."

"Just as you like," he answered, looking with some surprise at the car which stood waiting for Virginia, with its two immaculate servants. "It seems to me, dear," he added, with a note of disappointment in his tone, "that you have reached the end of your troubles without my help."

"I think I have, Guy," she answered, "but I am just as pleased to see you. Would you like to come and be introduced to my uncle and guardian?"

"Rather!" he answered.

"Back to Claridge's," she told the footman, and they stepped inside.

"This isn't a dream, is it?" Guy asked.

"I don't believe so," she answered. "You will find my uncle human enough, at any rate."

CHAPTER XXIII.
A DINNER PARTY

Phineas Duge in London was still a man of affairs. With a cigar in his mouth, and his hands behind his back, he was strolling about his handsomely furnished sitting-room at Claridge's, dictating to a secretary, while from an adjoining room came the faint click of a typewriter. Virginia entered somewhat unceremoniously, followed by Guy. Phineas Duge looked at them both in some surprise.

"Uncle," she said, "I met Guy coming away from Coniston Mansions. He was looking for me, and I have brought him to see you."

Phineas Duge held out his hand, and in obedience to a gesture, the secretary got up and left the room.

"I am very glad to meet you, sir," he said. "By the by, my niece has only mentioned your first name."

"I am the Duke of Mowbray," Guy said simply, "and I am very glad indeed to meet you if you are Virginia's uncle. I think that she treated me rather badly a week ago, but I am disposed," he added, with a twinkle in his eyes, "to be forgiving. I want your niece to be my wife, sir."

"Indeed!" Mr. Duge answered a little drily. "I can't say that I am glad to hear it, as I have only just discovered her myself."

"There is no reason, sir," Guy answered, "why you should lose her."

"You don't even know my uncle's name yet," Virginia said, smiling.

"I am Phineas Duge," Duge answered. "I dare say you have never heard of me. You see, I don't come often to England."

"Phineas Duge!" Guy gasped. "What, you mean the—?"

"Oh, yes! there is only one of us," Duge answered, smiling. "I am glad to hear that my fame, or perhaps my infamy, has reached even you."

Guy laughed.

"I don't think there is much question of infamy," he said. "I fancy that over here you will find yourself a very popular person indeed."

"Even," Phineas Duge answered, "although I allowed my niece to run away from home and come over here on a wild-goose chase. It was one of my mistakes, but Virginia has forgiven it. I suppose she has told you everything now."

"Everything," Guy answered, "and we should like to be married as soon as you will allow it."

"What about your people?" Duge asked.

Guy smiled.

"I fancy," he said, "that there will be no difficulty at all about that."

"You two," Phineas Duge said, "seem to have come across one another in a very unconventional manner, and yet, after all, it seems as though you were doing the thing which your people over here look upon at any rate with tolerance. I have only two girls to leave my millions to. You must send your solicitor to see me to-morrow."

"Virginia knows," Guy answered, "that I should be only too glad to have her without a sixpence."

"I myself am fond of money," Phineas Duge answered, smiling, "but I think that if I were your age I should feel very much the same."

"Uncle," Virginia said, "I have seen Mr. Vine and Stella, and I have given them your message. They are coming to dine with us at eight o'clock to-night. Couldn't we—couldn't—?"

Phineas Duge interrupted with a little shrug of the shoulders.

"Make it into a family party, I suppose you were going to say?" he remarked. "My niece hopes that you too will join us," he added, turning to the young man.

* * * * *

Guy raced back to Grosvenor Square. He found Lady Medlincourt playing bridge in the card-room.

"Aunt," he said, after having greeted her guests, "I must see you at once. Please come into the morning-room. I have something most important to say."

"If you dare to disturb me until I have finished this hand, I shall never speak to you again," she declared. "If we lose this rubber, my diamonds will have to go."

He walked about the room, trying to conceal his impatience. Fortunately Lady Medlincourt won the rubber, and having collected her winnings, she followed him into the morning-room.

"Well, Guy, what is it?" she said resentfully. "I suppose you have found that child?"

"I have not only found her," he answered, "but I have found out all about her. Do you know whose niece she is, and whom she is staying with?"

"How should I, my dear boy?" she answered.

"Her uncle is Phineas Duge," Guy said. "He has given his consent to our marriage, and told me to send my lawyer to him to-morrow."

"Bless the boy, what luck!" Lady Medlincourt exclaimed. "Why, he's the richest man in America."

Guy nodded.

"I don't care a bit," he said, "except that it will make all you people so much more decent to Virginia. Come along round to Claridge's and be introduced. There's just time."

The dinner-party that night was a great success. In the middle of it Lady Medlincourt laughed softly to herself.

"I must tell you all something," she said. "You know Guy went to America this year to see his cousin who is out ranching. He was so afraid that people would think he had gone out to find an American heiress—you know we're all disgracefully poor—that he stayed in New York, and came back, under an assumed name. In fact, he was only in New York for two days, for fear that some one should find him out. And to think, Guy," she exclaimed, "that you are going to do the conventional thing after all!"

"My dear lady," Phineas Duge said, "the conventions in your wonderful country are not things to be trifled with. Somehow or other they will assert themselves. There is your nephew here trying to prove to the world that he will have nothing to do with them, and yet it will be his painful duty to receive as much of my hard-earned savings as my daughter's dowry and Virginia's trousseau will leave to me. Never, until I was inveigled into Doucet's this afternoon, did I really understand the absolute recklessness of young women who are going to marry Englishmen."

Virginia laughed softly.

"What there is in me of extravagance," she said, laying her hand for a moment upon his arm, "I owe to you. Who else would have cabled to all my people to come over here for such an unimportant function as my wedding!"

Norris Vine caught his host's eye and raised his glass.

"May I be permitted," he asked, "to propose a toast—or rather several toasts? I drink with you, sir," he added, with a slight bow, "to the extinction of an ancient enmity! I have been something of a fanatic, I fear, as all those must be who take to their hearts a righteous cause. I drink to your charming niece, and to the fortunate young gentleman who is to be her husband! And lastly, I drink to our great country!"

"To America, and the extinction of all enmities!" Phineas Duge cried, holding his glass above his head.

"To America, and the sweetest of all her daughters!" Guy whispered in Virginia's ears.